Wicked
Izzy

Dale J. Young

ALSO BY DALE J. YOUNG

Horror novels:

The Darklands
The Ghost of Tobacco Road
Wicked Izzy

Other novels:

Hanging the Artificial Sun

This book is a work of fiction. Names, characters, places and incidents either are a product of the author's imagination or are used fictitiously. Any resemblance to actual persons, living or dead, events, or locales is entirely coincidental.

Thank you for purchasing this novel.

Acknowledgements

While a writer may write alone, a finished novel is never a one-person affair. Many people came together in the production of this novel. First and foremost, I would like to thank my wife for her unwavering support, and her compassion and understanding towards my obsession with the written word. And I'd like to send out a big thank you to all my beta readers, especially Cheryl and Heidi. Your sharp eyes make it much less likely that I will make a fool out of myself. I would also like to thank Debbie for the wonderful cover art, and to everyone else behind the scenes at Niner 8 Books.

To the lost souls…

PROLOGUE

November 1986

N ancy Stedford looked up at the full moon through the barren limbs of the trees surrounding the cemetery in the small hamlet of Solomon, NC. She bowed her head and pulled up the hood of her wool coat to shield herself from the cold wind as she walked towards the cemetery gate. It was close to midnight, and she knew she didn't have much time. The woman would meet her soon and despite her fear, Nancy knew this was what she wanted.

The wrought-iron gate groaned as she pulled it open and when she closed it behind her, the sound of the latch echoed off the tombstones. She looked out across the deserted cemetery and felt a glimmer of hope. It had been over a month since the accident, but the pain of her loss was still fresh and was now becoming more than she could bear. But if the stories were true, then tonight would bring relief, and a remedy for her pain and suffering.

Moving along the waist-high stone wall that surrounded the cemetery, she looked out across the field of lonely tombstones jutting out of the grass, each painted silver by the moonlight. She thought about all the people left behind to grieve for those lying underneath the stones. How many of them, their hearts laden with grief, had done what she was about to do? And how many of them had thought better of it.

Nancy moved along the footpath at the base of the wall until she came to the end of the row of tombstones she was looking for. She paused, closed her eyes and then pulled a deep breath of the cold November air into her lungs. When she opened her eyes, she felt a tiny flicker of strength ignite in her chest. Tonight, there would be relief from her misery, she thought as she walked down the row. When she came to a large, cross-shaped stone she stopped and felt sadness overcome her as she reached out and touched the cold granite.

"I love you so much," she whispered.

The sound of leaves rustling under foot startled Nancy as she looked up from the stone. She glanced to her right and saw the woman approaching from the far end of the row. A bolt of fear rushed through her body but she fought against the urge to turn and run. This was what she wanted and there was no need to change her mind now. The cold wind fingered her neck through the front of her hood and a shiver worked its way down her body. Suddenly the woman was upon her.

"My name is Isabelle Pearl," the woman said as she looked into Nancy's eyes.

Nancy felt her knees wobble and for a moment she thought she was going to faint. Then she felt a calm feeling wash over her. Something about the woman put her at ease.

Isabelle smiled. "I can give you what you crave so dearly."

Nancy trembled as she stood in front of the tombstone. "Then the stories are true," she said.

The wind lifted Isabelle's blonde hair away from her face. "They are true, but we must understand each other." Isabelle captured some of her wayward hair and pulled it behind her ear.

"I… I don't understand…" Nancy said.

Isabelle smiled, then spoke the words that would change Nancy Stedford's life forever.

"You must understand that what I offer you carries a price."

1

2010

JoAnna Stedford looked through the windshield of her car. "Small town America, or what's left of it," she said to herself as she turned off the main street of Bellville, SC, and onto the street that led to her husband Paul's old neighborhood. After several more turns she pulled up in front of his house, the place where he had grown up and where his life had changed forever at the age of twelve.

She brought the red Mercedes to a stop in front of the small brick rancher. A sign in the front yard read *For Sale. Bank Owned.* She glanced around nervously at the other houses but could see no other signs of life. Except for one house two doors down, most of the driveways were empty, and the neighborhood looked deserted.

JoAnna killed the engine and sat in the driver's seat for a few minutes, turning her head as she scanned the houses around her one more time to see if any of the window shades were moving. Even though the homes looked deserted, she still felt like someone was watching her. When she finally worked up the nerve to step out of her car, she walked up to the edge of the driveway and looked across the small front yard at the house.

Weeds poked through cracks in the driveway and she could see a lockbox hanging on the doorknob. To make it look as if she was interested in buying the house, she walked through the knee-high grass to the sign and pulled one of the sales flyers from the box attached to the pole.

Once on the front porch, she peeked through glass on each side of the door. Even though the yard had clearly not been maintained, the furniture inside house appeared to be undisturbed. After peering through the windows for a few minutes, she walked to the edge of the front porch and looked down the walkway towards the corner of the house. What she really wanted to see was the old shed where Paul's father had killed himself when Paul was twelve years old.

In the back corner of the yard, she found the shed surrounded by weeds with moss covering most of the roof. Next to the door of the shed was a solitary window, half open with one of the panes broken out. She felt her curiosity flare when she noticed the cracked open door.

JoAnna took one more look around and then stared at the paper in her hand pretending to read about the details of the house. Then she looked at the shed again. This is where she knew her journey would begin, at the place where Eli Stedford ended his life over a decade ago.

Paul had taken her to his house many times while they were dating but there had never been a reason to go into the old shed. At the time she didn't know that his father had committed suicide. He had revealed this dark secret to her while they were driving to the Outer Banks on their honeymoon over a year ago. Until that night, he had only told her that his father had died when he was twelve. He never gave her any details, and his mother had never mentioned it.

The wind whispered in the trees as JoAnna walked up to the shed. When she reached the door, she stopped and stood motionless in the tall grass while trying to find the courage to reach up and push the door open. The rusted hinges creaked in protest when she finally pushed on the door. Once her eyes adjusted, she scanned the interior.

Vandals and curious neighbors had long since removed most of the shed's contents. Only a rake and a shovel propped in the corner remained. Cheap indoor-outdoor carpet covered the floor and as JoAnna walked to the middle of the shed, she tried to imagine Paul finding his father's body in the wheelbarrow. But there were no stains on the carpet to indicate where it had been located.

JoAnna's eyes followed the carpet to the walls. Maybe someone had added it to the shed later, after the suicide, she thought as she reached down and peeled it back from the plywood floor. When she pulled the carpet back far enough to reveal a large, reddish-brown stain in the middle of the floor, she let go of it and took a step backwards, inhaling sharply. This had to be the place where Eli Stedford had killed himself with the shotgun. Paul had told her about his father's body in the wheelbarrow and how the blood had drained through a hole and onto the floor.

When a hand touched JoAnna's shoulder, she screamed and turned quickly to find herself staring into the eyes of a middle-aged woman. She had been so mesmerized by the sight of the bloodstain that she had not even heard the woman approach.

"You don't want this house," the woman said, her voice low and ominous. "Death is all around it."

JoAnna felt a flash of anger. "Good Lord, you scared me!" She stepped through the doorway of the shed and into the tall grass to put a few feet of distance in between her and the woman.

"Death is all around this house," the woman said again. JoAnna tried to collect herself before saying anything. Finally, she gained her composure.

"I… I don't want to buy the house. I was just looking around." JoAnna brought a hand to her forehead and tried to calm her nerves. "I knew the people that lived here. My mother-in-law owned this house. This is where my husband grew up."

Suddenly the old woman's face softened with recognition. "JoAnna? You're JoAnna Stedford?"

"How do you know my name?"

The old woman pointed to the house. "Nancy was a dear friend. We became good friends right after they moved in years ago, before Paul was born." Grief clouded the woman's face. "My husband is the one that found Nancy."

JoAnna felt relieved when she realized that the old woman wasn't a danger to her. This woman obviously knew Paul's family and maybe could help fill in the blanks about what had happened. Paul had told her about his father's suicide, but JoAnna knew next to nothing about what had happened to his mother Nancy.

The woman smiled. "I remember you. My name is Lynette. I live next door. I remember meeting you several years ago when Paul brought you to his house. I was over visiting with his mother when you two walked in." JoAnna searched her memory but could not remember meeting the woman.

Lynette looked at the shed and then at the house. "So sad what happened here…" Then she looked at JoAnna. "Say, would you like a cup of coffee?"

JoAnna knew that she should probably be on her way and that at any moment her mother would call to check on her progress. But she knew that Lynette would be able to tell her everything she wanted to know about Paul's mother.

"Well, a cup of coffee would be nice. I can only stay a minute though. I'm on my way to the coast."

The two women walked to the back door of Lynette's house. JoAnna sat down at the kitchen table while Lynette poured two cups of coffee. She sat one in front of JoAnna and then went to the cupboard for the sugar and creamer.

Lynette sat down at the table and placed her hand on top of JoAnna's. "I was so sorry to hear about Paul. I just don't know what to say. He always talked about how lucky he was to have found you. I just don't know why he would do something like what he did."

JoAnna took a sip of her coffee. "Thank you. I'm still coming to grips with it myself. But I'm getting better." She looked at Lynette and tried to smile. "Can you tell me about Paul's mother? What happened to her?" Lynette leaned back in her chair and folded her arms in front of her, then placed a hand on her cheek as the memories started coming back.

"It was hard enough on Nancy for her husband to commit suicide right out there in that shed. I guess you saw the stain on the floor. I never understood why she didn't have that thing torn down. Just never understood it." Lynette looked out the window. "Poor little Paul found his daddy's body out there lying in a wheelbarrow with a load of buckshot in his chest. If it had been up to me, I'm telling you I would have had it torn down."

JoAnna nodded. "Me too."

Lynette sighed and took a sip of coffee. "That poor boy was only twelve years old. But looking back, I think Paul seemed to get over it better than Nancy did. Sometimes kids are like that. But Nancy was never the same. Always sad, and that just broke my heart. I tried to be the best friend I could to her, tried to help her, but she was just never the same. The only time I ever saw her brighten up was when Paul met you. She seemed to think that maybe he would have a better life than she did because he had you. I just don't understand why that boy followed his father to the grave."

JoAnna reached out and patted Lynette's hand. "I'm sure you were a good friend to her. But sometimes people just can't recover from something like that. Most of the time they can, but sometimes they just can't. Sometimes a suicide just feels so much like a betrayal to the ones left behind that they just can't take it."

Lynette smiled understandingly and continued. "Then one day about a year ago, right after she came back from Charleston and burying Paul, she just up and disappeared. We didn't see any signs of life at her house. Her car didn't move for days. Finally, my husband took the spare key Nancy had given us and went over to check on her. He found her in the bathtub with a revolver in her lap. She had put the barrel in her mouth and pulled the trigger." Lynette's eyes watered as she covered her mouth with her hand.

JoAnna looked down at the table as her heart flooded with sorrow. This was obviously painful for Lynette but she wanted to hear what the woman had to say. She didn't want her to stop talking.

"My husband came home pale in the face and told me to call 911. He wouldn't let me go over to the house. All I ever saw was her body in a bag on the stretcher when the paramedics brought her out. My husband was right to make me stay home. I'm glad I didn't go over there."

"Did anyone have a theory about why she killer herself? Did she leave a note?" JoAnna asked.

Lynette looked down at her coffee mug and nodded. "She left a note."

Trying to be as gentle as she could, JoAnna asked, "can you tell me what it said?"

Lynette raised her eyes. Part of her wondered about JoAnna's curiosity, but then she reminded herself that Nancy had been her mother-in-law so her curiosity was understandable.

"The note said it was all her fault."

JoAnna frowned. "Her fault?"

"I never understood what she meant. The note said that she just couldn't handle the grief of losing her son and husband. But then it said that everything was her fault."

"I don't understand," JoAnna said, before taking a sip of her coffee.

"I don't either. I was Nancy's friend from the time they moved into that house until her death. They came from some town in North Carolina, somewhere in the eastern part of the state. I can't remember the name of it. Nancy told me once but I've forgotten it, and after that she never much talked about their life before moving here. She just said something about her husband wanting to work at the paper mill here in town. He was some kind of maintenance man or something. We became good friends after they moved in and she was always such a sweet lady, but I never could get any details out of her about their life before moving here. I just quit asking after a while. I guess it really didn't matter, anyway. It was none of my business."

JoAnna looked through the window at the shed again and then turned to Lynette. "They're from a little town named Solomon. Paul told me that when we were dating. He overheard his parents talking about it when he was little but the name was the only thing he remembered. Nancy and Eli were born there but Paul said they never took him back to visit relatives. We drove right through it on the way the Outer Banks on our honeymoon, but I don't remember it because I was asleep. He never said much about it after that."

"Solomon? I've never heard of it," Lynette said.

"Me neither, until Paul told me about it."

JoAnna didn't want to give Lynette the details about her trip to the coast so she decided to redirect the conversation back to the suicide note.

"And Nancy said it was her fault."

"Yep," replied Lynette. "Makes no sense... She said everything was her fault. I took it to mean that included Paul." Lynette paused for a few seconds before speaking again. When she finally spoke, her voice was barely above a whisper. "And there was something else in the note."

"Something else?"

"She... Well, I've never been able to figure out what it meant."

"Tell me, Lynette. Maybe I can help."

Lynette looked at JoAnna, her eyes full of tears. She wiped her face with a tissue and looked through the window at Nancy's house, but to JoAnna it seemed that Lynette was looking past the house into the distance.

"In the note..." Lynette sniffled and wiped her nose with the tissue. "In the note, the last thing Nancy said was that it was hard enough on her to lose her husband the first time and that she just couldn't take it again."

JoAnna leaned back in her chair. "Hard enough the first time? What does that mean?" She looked through the window at the old shed, then asked the only question that made any sense. "Had she ever been married before? Maybe Eli was her second husband."

Lynette shook her head. "She never mentioned a previous husband. She told me once that she and Eli got married right after they got out of high school, so I doubt she was married before that."

JoAnna turned her gaze from the back window and the shed to the side window of Lynette's kitchen. "What's going on with their house?"

"Bank took it. Nancy had no relatives, or at least if she did none of them came forward. The poor woman didn't even have anyone to bury her. The county came in and paid to have her cremated, like they do with vagrants and homeless people, then the bank foreclosed on the house and stuck a sign in the yard. Right before they did, a truck showed up one day and some men went inside to do some work. I assumed they were cleaning up the bathroom where Nancy killed herself. The house has been for sale ever since but no one ever comes to look at it. Word gets out, you know. No one is going to buy a house where two people committed suicide. The bank has even stopped having the grass cut. I think they've just given up on it. It wouldn't surprise me if they end up tearing it down."

Lynette fumbled with her tissue and then wiped her eyes and nose. "It was just so sad. Nancy had Eli cremated and had his ashes thrown in the Congaree River. There was a funeral but hardly anyone came to it. I remember how heartbroken little Paul was. They cremated Eli the next day. Nancy handled it all by herself as if it was a big secret or something. She just didn't want to bury that man for some reason. And then when the county cremated her and disposed of her ashes, where I have no idea, it wiped away all traces of them. I didn't even have a grave to go to so I could pay my respects. As far as I know, the only one in that family that has a grave is Paul."

"Yes, we buried Paul in Charleston." JoAnna felt her heart skip in her chest. "He wasn't cremated. I thought about it but just couldn't do it. I remember his mother suggesting it, which I found odd, but the decision was mine and I just couldn't do it."

Lynette dabbed at her eyes again. "It's always best to have somewhere to go to lay flowers."

The two women sat in silence for a few minutes. JoAnna was at a loss for words but she was glad she had accepted Lynette's offer for coffee. The story from Lynette held exactly the kind of details she wanted to know. It had answered questions for her, but it had also raised other ones. Why would Nancy Stedford think everything was her fault? And what did she mean about it being hard enough losing her husband the first time?

They talked for a few more minutes about the neighborhood and how it was in decline. People were moving away because jobs were getting scarce and the neighborhood was falling into disrepair. There was even talk of the paper mill closing. Lynette told JoAnna that would be the death of Bellville. The paper mill was about the only company in town that paid a decent wage and if it went, there would be a wave of foreclosures and the town would go under.

When they finished their coffee, JoAnna rose from the table and gave Lynette a hug. She thanked her for her time and for sharing the painful details of Nancy's final days. Once back in the Mercedes, she dialed her mother on the cellphone to check in, figuring it was best if she called first. Once she had her mother on the line, she lied to her and told her that she was already in North Carolina and well on her way to the Outer Banks. She didn't tell Maxine about her trip to Bellville and about meeting Lynette.

Once she ended the call, JoAnna set the cruise control on the Mercedes and eased back in her seat for the ride to Greenville, NC. Once there, she would exit the Interstate in favor of the lonely road through the marshlands that she and Paul had taken on their honeymoon trip. The first stage of her trip had been a success even though it made her sad to hear Lynette's story. She fiddled with the knob on the radio before giving up and turning the volume down. In the back of her mind, she knew that the dark secrets Lynette had revealed to her were only the beginning of the story of her husband's family, and that even darker ones lay ahead. Perhaps she would find the answers to some of these secrets once she got to Solomon.

2

It took JoAnna a few hours to reach Greenville. After filling the tank of her car with gas, she went to the restroom and walked down one of the long isles full of snacks. The truck stop was a busy place, and she felt secure knowing there were lots of people around her.

Once she paid for her snacks and gas, she went back to the Mercedes. When she got back in the car, she screwed off the lid of her bottle of Coke and took a few long sips. Then she ripped open her bag of peanuts and poured them into the bottle.

"Mmmmm," she said after she took a sip and crunched some of the peanuts. The salty, sweet mix brought back memories and when she looked over at the seat beside her a wave of sorrow washed over her. The empty seat reminded her of how much she missed her husband.

JoAnna screwed the lid back onto the Coke and then placed it in the cup holder between the seats. She thought about calling her mother to check in again but decided against it. She would call her as soon as she got to her hotel for the night. It was getting late in the afternoon and she planned to keep her promise to her mother and be off the highway by nine in the evening. It was the least she could do since her mother had been so cooperative.

The old map was one of the few things she had managed to save from their honeymoon trip and when she pulled it out of her purse, she felt another pang of sorrow crawl through her chest. She remembered how they had chosen to use the old paper map in favor of the GPS just to have a keepsake from their trip. She looked down at it as she ran her hand across the soft surface thinking back about how they had huddled over the map in Paul's old car, tracing the lines and plotting their trip. On that day they had their whole lives in front of them. Now it was all gone.

JoAnna unfolded the map and traced the line of State Road 23 leading from Greenville towards Pamlico Sound. When her finger traced the red line that crossed Lake Mattamuskeet, a special memory came to mind. She figured that she could make it down State Road 23, cut across Lake Mattamuskeet and then make it to Solomon by nine o'clock.

Once back on the road, she traveled east on 23 and before long came to the town of Washington. She drove through the town without stopping and once on the other side the road narrowed and civilization dissipated. She chided herself for not stopping in Washington to go to the restroom. Having no other choice, she pulled into a small gas station that was not nearly as inviting as the large truck stop in Greenville, but she had no other choice. It was either go to the restroom in the gas station or on the side of the road. This was the price she had to pay for enjoying her large bottle of Coke and peanuts.

The old gas station doubled as a tackle shop. Several long, yellow neon lights buzzed above the front door while a Budweiser sign flashed in the window. There were no other cars in the lot so JoAnna parked close to the front door so that she would not have far to walk. When she got out of the Mercedes, the familiar smell of swamp air invaded her nostrils. It stirred emotions in her that had been dormant for a long time.

A small bell jingled when she pulled open the door, alerting the young man sitting behind the cash register. A ball cap shaded his unshaven face, and his shirt had grease spots on it. He was reading some sort of magazine and barely noticed JoAnna as she walked through the door. She nodded at the young man and then scanned the rest of the store. It was just the two of them.

The first thing JoAnna noticed in the bathroom was the smell, and then the condom machine on the wall. A lone toilet sat in the corner next to a sink that she guessed hadn't been cleaned in years. She dropped her jeans and hovered over the toilet seat, careful to only touch it with her hands. She frowned at the empty toilet paper dispenser and then at the air dryer on the wall next to the sink.

Once out of the restroom she noticed the young man behind the counter was gone. A bolt of panic stabbed her abdomen as she looked around the interior of the empty store. The man was nowhere in sight. She had planned to purchase another drink, just as compensation for using the restroom, but decided against it. When she walked outside, she found him standing next to the Mercedes on the passenger side, admiring the car.

"This is a nice one," he said while rubbing the stubble on his cheeks. "I towed a Mercedes a few weeks ago, but it wasn't as nice as this one. That's some kind of red, ain't it?" The young man looked at JoAnna and smiled. The nametag on his shirt labeled him as Danny.

"Um, yeah. It is a pretty red," JoAnna stammered as she fumbled with her key fob trying to find the button on the remote to unlock the door. She knew that the best thing for her to do was to not show any fear. If Danny was someone she needed to worry about, the last thing she wanted to do was come across as a frightened, helpless girl.

"I was going to buy a drink since I used your restroom, but I came out and you were gone. I'm on my way to visit some relatives and they're expecting me, so I'm kind of in a hurry. I'll just get a drink some other time." JoAnna finally found the button on the remote and was careful to only push it once so that it only unlocked the driver's side door.

"You going down 23?" replied Danny as he looked down the long highway leading away from his gas station. JoAnna knew better than to tell the young man where she was actually going, but highway 23 was the only road out of town so she could hardly lie to him.

"Yes, I'm on my way down 23," she said, hoping he wouldn't press for details. At first, Danny just stood up straight and looked at her. Then his eyes grew wide and his face clouded over.

"Into the swamps?"

"Well… Yes. The road does go through the swamps." JoAnna opened her car door and placed one foot in the floorboard. Danny looked down the highway again and then back at her.

"Stay on the main road. Don't take any side roads or anything like that. Just stay on 23 until you get wherever you're going." He paused and looked JoAnna in the eyes. "Stay on the main road."

With this, Danny stepped backwards until he was in front of the door to the store. JoAnna looked at him for a second. "Thanks." She wasn't sure of what to make of what he had just said to her. She sat down in the seat, closed the door and hit the lock button. When she looked up at Danny, he waved at her and then went back into the store. She watched him through the glass as walked to his place behind the cash register, then she put the Mercedes in reverse and backed away.

Within seconds JoAnna had the Mercedes up to speed on highway 23. It was fall of the year and the air was cool and scented with the smell of pine trees, and the sky above the tree line was the color of burnished copper. She rolled down the windows and then fiddled with the buttons on the steering wheel that controlled the radio until she found a station playing classic rock. She remembered how she and Paul had not been able to find much on the old FM radio in his car when they were traveling through the swamps on their honeymoon trip.

JoAnna breathed in the air, heavy with the aroma of trees and stagnant water. Her hair ambled in the breeze as it rolled through the Mercedes and she found herself remembering Paul and the time when they were on this very same highway at almost the exact same time of night. She felt a pang of heartache as she realized that driving on the same road made her yearn for him more than ever.

She knew this was supposed to be a farewell trip to the life she had lived before his death. The plan was to allow herself to miss him, to remember the good times they had shared, and to see some of the places they had gone to together on their honeymoon. And when the trip was over, she would say goodbye to all of it and start her life over again. This was what she had told her mother, anyway. She hadn't told her mother that what she really wanted to do was to find Solomon and see if it held any secrets about Paul's family. And if it turned out that there were no secrets to find, then perhaps she would do exactly what she had told her mother she would do. But in her heart, she realized she would never be able to get over Paul and that he would haunt her memory forever.

After driving for a while, JoAnna lost track of the time. She passed through the small hamlet of Arcadia and wanted to stop to get something to drink or maybe even a bite to eat but she had not seen any fast-food restaurants, or even a small diner when passing through the town. There were only a few vacant stores, a gas station closed for the night, and a small, brightly lit used car lot. She had not even seen a drink machine outside any of the buildings, not that she would have stopped to use it if she had. The farther she traveled into the backcountry the more she was starting to feel that the best thing for her to do was to just keep driving until she reached a hotel.

Once she left Arcadia, the streetlights ended. There were no cars in her rearview mirror and none coming toward her in the distance. State Road 23 was now just a narrow band of blacktop bordered on each side by dark stands of trees poking out of the swamp water. The surrounding darkness weighed heavy and reminded her of how crazy it was for her to be out on the road all by herself. But the desire to find out about Paul's family was strong, so strong in fact that she had a hard time understanding it. For some odd reason, she felt like she had to be out here, that she really had no choice in the matter. Maybe she was just tired and not thinking straight, but she couldn't shake the feeling that her destiny was set, and that there was no way to turn back even if she wanted to.

She reached for her cellphone and called her mother to check in. They chatted for a few minutes and she told her mother that she was probably about an hour away from stopping for the night. This made Maxine happy and after a few minutes she told JoAnna to call her when she was in her hotel for the night.

The radio crackled and then lost the distant channel. As she fiddled with the knob and tried to find another station, she couldn't understand how her mother could pay so much for a car but not pay for a satellite radio subscription. Then she looked up from the dial and gasped when she saw a man standing in the middle of the road.

She closed her eyes and jammed her foot down on the brake pedal. The expensive tires on the Mercedes screamed in protest as the car skidded to a halt. When she opened her eyes again, the man was gone. Paralyzed by fear, she tried to calm her nerves as she searched for the man in the circle of light in front of the car. But he was nowhere to be found. She looked out of the side windows and in the rearview mirror but there was nothing but inky darkness around her.

Once back up to speed, she tried to put the image of the man out of her mind by thinking about Lynette and the trip to Bellville. Lynette's story about the Stedford family was strange, and JoAnna thought about how Paul had never given her any details about where his family was from. In all their years of dating, and during their year of marriage he had never said anything about where his mother and father grew up, who his grandparents were, or anything else about his family's roots. Not a word. She had never met anyone before who didn't at least say a little about their grandparents. All he knew was the name of the town where his parents were born, and nothing more.

The heavy swamp air calmed her nerves as it circulated through the car. More memories of Paul danced through her mind as the car cut through the darkness, then her mind returned to Bellville. She remembered Lynette saying Nancy never gave up any details other than the one time she named the town. Why the big secret? Who hides their background like that?

Her mind drifted back and forth from Lynette to memories of her honeymoon trip with Paul. She remembered how they had laughed and joked about the swamp creatures that were lurking in the darkness as they drove past. A mischievous grin crossed her face when she thought about having sex on the dark, deserted bridge across Lake Mattamuskeet. It was one of her favorite memories from a night she knew she would never forget.

3

The road sign floated in the darkness ahead. When JoAnna got closer, she read the words bathed in the white light of her headlights. *Welcome to Solomon, NC.* She slowed down to around twenty-five miles an hour knowing that the last thing she needed was a speeding ticket from a small-town sheriff's deputy. She passed under several streetlights before seeing a small house to her left with a sign out front that read *Madam Valentine, Psychic and Palm Reader.* The house was dark, and no cars were in the small gravel parking lot.

On the right was a small diner, also closed for the night. "A BLT and some sweet tea would hit the spot right now," JoAnna mumbled as she rolled past. Next to the diner sat a small motel with one car in the parking lot. The sign out front read *Swamp Fox Inn* in bright yellow neon with *vacancy* flashing underneath.

A grin crossed her face when she read the sign. "Every town has a no-tell motel," she said to herself. She remembered how Paul had always tried to talk her into stopping at seedy roadside motels every time they went on a trip together. He always told her the best sex in the world was in a "no-tell motel", as he called them, with the drapes drawn and the car right outside the door. She remembered how they once had taken a trip to the mountains when they were dating and she had finally given in to his urge. Just for fun they had pretended they were complete strangers and that had just met in a bar. The sex had been incredible, and she had told him afterwards how ashamed she was of herself but that she wouldn't mind doing it again.

JoAnna wanted to stop for the night but the Swamp Fox Inn gave her the heebies, and she figured that maybe a better motel was just down the road. She decided to drive just a little further to see what else she could find, but when the street lights ended and the blackness of the swamp night closed in around her, she knew there probably weren't any other motels around. When she saw a dimly lit sign ahead, she slowed down and watched as an old gas station drifted by.

She thought about the gas station and wondered if it was the one Paul had stopped at on the night of their honeymoon trip. She had been asleep at the time and later he told her that the owner, an old man with a large Rottweiler, had stepped out of the darkness to confront him, thinking he was a vandal. Paul was able to make peace with the old man and then get a drink from the machine, but had told her later that the old man seemed strange and that the dog had scared the hell out of him. It had to be the station Paul had told her about. She hadn't seen another one like it in town.

Thousands of stars twinkled in the moonless sky above the tree line. She leaned forward to see them and thought about how nice it would be if Paul was with her, comforting her and telling her everything would be okay. But as she looked up at the stars, she knew she was alone, and that Paul was gone forever. She could feel the pressure building in her eyes as she fought the urge to cry.

When JoAnna saw the man standing in the middle of the road, she gasped and gripped the steering wheel hard with both hands. She slammed on the brakes and turned the wheel hard to the right to avoid hitting him. This sent the Mercedes off the road and towards the swamp canal lying in front of the tree line. As her car left the pavement, she closed her eyes and clinched her teeth. Images flashed through her mind of her childhood, college and then of meeting Paul. She knew she could no longer control the car and that in a matter of seconds she would be in the swamp canal, sinking into the black water where no one would ever find her.

The front tires blew out as the car skidded sideways towards the swamp canal. JoAnna let out a scream as the car slid down the embankment and stopped a few feet shy of the edge of the canal.

Panic engulfed her as she fumbled with her seatbelt. Once she released it, she scrambled to the opposite side of the car and clawed at the door latch. When she finally got the door open, she fell out of the car and onto the ground. The edge of the canal was only a few feet away from her and she could see the surface of the black water lying still in the night.

Careful not to fall into the water, JoAnna pulled herself up and then stood behind the Mercedes keeping the car between herself and the road. She looked across the roof at the pool of light spilling onto the road from the headlights and saw that the man she had swerved to avoid was gone. Her emotions gave way. Sobbing uncontrollably, she slid down the side of the car until she was sitting on the ground with her back against the tire. After a few moments, she pulled her knees close to her chest and looked out over the black water at the stars reflecting off the glassy surface. A fish splashed in the distance. Then she heard a vehicle stop on the road, and the sound of approaching footsteps.

"You okay, missy? Are ya hurt?"

JoAnna froze at the sound of the voice. She turned her head and looked over the open passenger door at the man standing beside the front of her car, his shape silhouetted by the glow from the headlights. He held a flashlight in his hand and its beam suddenly caught her in the eyes.

"Are ya hurt?" the old man repeated. She remained silent as she squinted into the beam of the flashlight.

"I'm saying it one more time, missy. Are ya hurt?" Finally, JoAnna found the courage to speak.

"N… No…" Relief bloomed insider her as she realized the man standing at the front of her car apparently meant her no harm. "No. I'm fine," she repeated as she rose to her feet. When she did, she saw the flatbed wrecker parked by the side of the road, the beams from its red lights fingering the trees on the other side of the road. The old man pushed the passenger door shut and extended his hand.

"You better get away from that water. If you fall in, you're done for and I'm too old to go in after you."

JoAnna looked down at her feet and realized that only a step separated her from the edge of the canal. She reached over and took the old man's hand as he led her to the front of the car. Once they were in front of the headlights, she got a good look at him. A ball cap perched at an angle sat above his craggy, wrinkled face. His weathered hand held the flashlight while the other reached up and removed the stub of the cigarette pinched between his lips. A flick of his finger sent the stub flying towards the canal water.

"I saw you go off the road. I had just gone out to lock my pumps for the night when I saw you drive past. When I heard your tires squeal, I went back in and got my keys and came as fast as I could."

"Oh, thank you!" JoAnna leaned against the front of the car to get her bearings. "I can't thank you enough."

"The name's Raymond Greenfield. Everybody in town calls me Ray."

"My name is JoAnna. JoAnna Stedford."

Ray stepped back and pointed his flashlight at the car. "Well then, Miss Stedford," he said as his flashlight traced circles over the front tires, "I think you need to thank your lucky stars that you didn't go into that canal. The old finishing mill used to float small barges down this canal back in the day. They ain't exactly shallow if you follow what I'm sayin'. That canal would swallow your whole car." After he said this, Ray bent down on one knee and pointed his flashlight underneath the front end of the car.

"Is it bad?" JoAnna said, almost afraid to ask.

"Looks like those tree stumps only blew your tires, but they weren't tall enough to tear up your car underneath so you're in luck. The state came through here not long ago and cleared the trees along the canal. The stumps tore holes in your front tires. Not gonna be able to patch something like that. You'll need new ones."

JoAnna felt relieved. Ruining tires was one thing, tearing up her mother's car was another.

"Can you help me?" JoAnna said as Ray got back to his feet. "Can you help me get new tires? Do you sell them at your station?" Ray turned off his flashlight and dropped it in the pocket of his overalls, then removed his hat and rubbed his chin.

"Don't have any tires like these. I got mostly truck tires at my place. People in this town don't usually drive fancy cars like this. Pickup trucks, mostly. I can give you a tow over to Jared's garage. He might have some tires that will work but I doubt it. Probably have to send for them from Washington or Greenville. Might take him a day or two."

JoAnna felt her heart sink. What was she going to tell her mother? Should she call the insurance company? She had no idea what to do. Ray looked at her face and could tell she was upset.

"Missy, it ain't all that bad. I'll give you a tow over to Jared's and we'll leave your car there for the night. There's a motel on the way, and I'll drop you off there after we leave your car at Jared's. You can get a room and talk to Jared in the morning. I've known him for years and I'll make sure he treats you right."

JoAnna looked at Ray and smiled. "I saw it. The Swamp Fox Inn, I believe it was called?" She chuckled and wiped her eyes with the back of her hand.

Ray smiled at her opinion of the motel. "Well it ain't fancy but it's all we got. You'll be okay. Just lock your door."

"I'm sure it will be fine. I really appreciate your help."

"A tow is fifty dollars," Ray said, rubbing his chin again. He noticed the look on JoAnna's face and then reconsidered his price. "But I'm sayin' for you it's only twenty. Young girl out here all by herself on the highway, just about went into the canal, tore up your car. I'm sayin' you probably deserve a discount."

A smile crossed JoAnna's face. "Thank you so much, Mr. Greenfield."

"Everybody in town calls me Ray."

"Thank you so much, Ray."

"One more thing before I pick up your car. Why did you skid off the road? Were you trying to miss an animal?" Ray stepped back and surveyed the car and then he looked over at the road as if he might see something lying in it that would make a driver swerve off the road.

JoAnna thought for a second and knew that she had to invent a story. There was no way she was going to tell Ray that she swerved to miss a man standing in the road.

"I think it was a deer," she said, lying to Ray. "It was big and had horns. I knew if I hit it that it would have probably totaled my car."

"Horns?" Ray tried not to laugh.

"Antlers, I mean." JoAnna felt herself blush.

Ray looked back at the swamp canal. "Well, it's a good thing you got your car stopped before you went into that canal. Like I said, it ain't shallow. And there are things living in that water that would scare a young girl like you out of her wits."

JoAnna crossed her arms and looked at the dark canal. "I can imagine."

With this Ray walked off to his wrecker. In less than a minute he was backing down the grassy embankment towards the car. It took him less than fifteen minutes to hook up to it and pull it up onto the flatbed of the wrecker. Once he had the car secured, he and JoAnna climbed into the cab and began their ride to Jared's garage. She stared silently at the Swamp Fox Inn as they drove by and was sure her mother would not approve of her spending the night in such a place.

As Ray slowed the wrecker down and prepared to turn left onto the road that led to Jared's garage, JoAnna looked over to her right and saw the dark house with the sign out front advertising palm reading. She decided to strike up a conversation about it.

"Of all the things for a little town like this to have, I'd have never guessed it would be a palm reader." As Ray turned the steering wheel of the wrecker, he glanced over his right shoulder and looked at the house.

"That's Cassandra Valentine's place. She likes for people to call her Madam Valentine. She'll read your palm and tell you things about yourself that you don't want to know. I'm sayin' she knows things, things of a personal nature."

JoAnna looked back at the dark house as they turned down the side street. "Really?" she said, feigning amazement. She considered palm reading a hoax. Ray picked up on this and grinned as he adjusted his hat.

"If you get bored tomorrow while waiting on your tires maybe you can go see her. I'm sayin' just for fun, you know. There's not much else to do around this old town."

JoAnna laughed. "I'd have to be pretty bored but I'll think about it."

When they pulled into Jared's garage, Ray turned the wrecker around and backed up to the corner of the parking lot, then got out and lowered the car to the pavement. JoAnna retrieved her bags and then got back in the wrecker. Once he was behind the wheel again, Ray reached into his shirt pocket and handed her a pen, then fumbled in the console until he found a half empty book of matches. He pointed to the phone number painted on the door to the garage's office.

"Write that phone number down so you can call Jared in the morning. Tell him Ray brought your car over here. Tell him I said to give you the local's price and not the out-of-towner's price for his work."

JoAnna scribbled the number on the flap of the book of matches. "I will definitely tell him that. Thank you again for all this." Ray put the wrecker in gear and a few seconds later they were on their way to the Swamp Fox Inn. JoAnna shuddered at the thought of the place, and at the idea of having to tell her mother about it. She was already dreading the call, and what she knew would be a long, lonely night.

4

When Ray pulled up to the Swamp Fox Inn, there was still only one other car in the parking lot. JoAnna didn't know if it was the night clerk's car or the car of a guest. She hoped it was a guest's car so that she wouldn't be the only person staying for the night. When Ray brought the wrecker to a stop, she looked at the front office and then back at him.

"Well, this is where I get off. Thank you again for the help." She fumbled in her purse and produced a twenty-dollar bill, then tried to hand it to Ray. But he kept his hands on the steering wheel and didn't reach for the bill.

"Maybe you should just keep that. I'm sayin' the tow is free. Young girl out here on the highway all by herself, car broken down, gotta stay in a roadside dive for the night… You ought to be home with people that love you, not out here in the country, and especially not in a town like Solomon."

"Oh no, really. Please take the money, Ray. You were very generous to lower your price in the first place so please let me pay you." JoAnna extended her arm, hoping he would take the money.

"I'm sayin' the tow is free, missy. It's the least I can do. Young girl out here alone… It just ain't right. And it just ain't right that you gotta stay in this motel here either, but it's all we got. You just keep your door locked, you understand? Have you got a gun with you?"

JoAnna stammered. "A gun? Uh… no, I don't have a gun."

"It figures." Ray adjusted his hat. "I'm saying keep your doors locked."

JoAnna looked at the row of doors extending down the front of the motel and swallowed the lump in her throat. "You can count on that, Mr. Greenfield."

"It's Ray."

"You can count on that, Ray. I will definitely lock my door. I'll probably wedge a chair underneath the doorknob too."

"That's a good idea, missy."

JoAnna turned the door handle and opened the door. When she stepped down onto the gravel, she could see the look of apprehension in the old man's dark eyes.

"You take care, missy."

JoAnna nodded and thanked Ray again for his help. She pulled her duffel bag out of the floorboard, shut the door and then walked to the office. When she opened the door, a small bell jingled. She walked up to the front desk and sat her bag down beside her as she listened to the sound of Ray pulling away in his truck.

"Good evening," the night man said as he walked out of a small office behind the front desk. "What can I do for you?"

To JoAnna, this was a ridiculous question. Was there any other reason to be standing in a motel front office in the middle night other than to rent a room? The night man stepped up to the counter and smiled. He was a young man with brown hair and hazel-green eyes, and JoAnna guessed him to be in his early thirties.

"I'd like a room for the night."

"Well you've come to the right place." His lips curled at the edges. "My name is Cooper. I'm the night manager. We aim to please here at the Swamp Fox Inn. Let me see what I have available."

Cooper turned and looked at the full rack of keys hanging behind him before finally choosing one. JoAnna frowned when he laid the old-fashioned key on the counter.

"There we go. Room 101. Right down at the end. The rate is forty-five dollars a night, two nights for eighty."

"I'll just need tonight." JoAnna pulled the money from her purse. She didn't like the idea of handing her credit card to the night man so she opted for cash instead.

"That's forty-five dollars a night per person, I should say." Cooper looked through the front door at the empty parking lot.

"I'm alone." JoAnna felt her forehead heat from the mix of embarrassment and fear.

"Well, that will be forty-five then. Two nights for eighty. Just in case you need to stay another night." A grin spread across Cooper's face.

"I'll be leaving tomorrow," JoAnna replied indignantly. "I just need a room for tonight. And do you have one closer to the office?"

"Can't give you one of the closer rooms," replied Cooper. "East Pamlico keeps a block of rooms reserved in case they need them for visiting management. They get the close ones. But that room down on the end is nice and clean. You'll like it. I'll even throw in a free continental breakfast." He motioned at the coffee pot sitting on a small table in the corner of the office. "The diner always sends over a box of donuts every morning."

JoAnna looked at the coffee pot. It was sitting on a table next to a Christmas tree that looked as if it stayed up all year long. "Sounds wonderful." She reached over and took the key, dismayed again that it wasn't a modern cardkey. "What time is check out?"

Cooper's face darkened. "Noon. But like I said, you can have two nights for eighty dollars. That's a ten-dollar savings. If you decide to stay one more night, I'll still give you the discount rate."

JoAnna forced a smile. "Thanks. But I'm just staying because my car is being worked on over at Jared's garage. It should be ready tomorrow and I'll leave once I get it back."

"Suit yourself." Cooper closed the registry book in front of him. "Good night."

"Good night." JoAnna was sure that she had just offended the man. To make up for it, she motioned back at the coffee pot when she got to the front door. "Thanks for the donuts and coffee offer. I may take you up on it."

Cooper smiled and his face brightened. "You're welcome."

JoAnna stepped out into the cool night air. She glanced at the empty gravel parking lot as she walked quickly down the length of the motel to the room at the end. She looked over her shoulder to make sure no one was approaching as she tried to get the key in the lock. Since her room was on the end of the building, she could see the area behind the motel. The same swamp canal she had almost driven into passed behind the building, bordered by thick woods on the far side. Once inside her room, she reached beside the door and flicked the light switch. A solitary lamp beside the double bed came to life, illuminating the small room with a yellowish glow. She locked and bolted the door, then pushed over the little metal arm to activate the privacy lock.

She tossed her duffel bag on the bed and sat down beside it dreading the idea of having to call her mother. "Mom can wait a few more minutes," she said to the bag as if it were a companion. Then she got up and walked over to the vanity mirror. Just as she leaned in to examine her face, someone knocked on her door.

Turning to face the room, she backed up against the vanity and reached again for her nail file. "Yes?" she said, her voice weak. She cleared her throat and answered again, this time louder. "Who is it?"

"It's Cooper."

JoAnna walked to the door. What in the world could Cooper want? She had already paid him in cash for the room. When she got close to the door, Cooper spoke again. "It's Cooper, from the front office, Miss Stedford."

JoAnna opened the door a few inches until the privacy lock caught it.

"Can I help you?"

"Just thought you might want some extra towels."

She looked over her shoulder at the towel rack near the sink. She hadn't noticed until just now that it contained only one towel.

"Um... Yes... Thank you. If you could just set them down, I'll get them in a few minutes." She knew better than to open the door.

"Well... Okay, then." Cooper looked down at the stack of towels in his hands. "I'll just set them right here." He bent down and sat them beside the door, then stood up and looked at JoAnna peering at him through the crack in the door.

"If you need anything, anything at all, you just give me a ring. Just dial zero on the phone and it will ring my desk." JoAnna felt a spark of fear in her stomach when his eyes left hers and moved down her body.

"Anything at all," he said when his eyes returned to hers. Then he turned and walked off.

JoAnna closed the door and locked the deadbolt. She let out a breath as she leaned forward and felt the cool steel of the door touch her forehead. *What are you doing here, JoAnna Stedford?* She tried to force the question out of her mind but the nagging thought that her trip was quickly turning into a nightmare would not go away. She checked the locks on the door once again and then went to the edge of the bed and sat down. It was time to call her mother.

An old rotary-type phone sat on the nightstand. She had not seen one like since her childhood. She pulled her cellphone from her purse and while she waited for her mother to answer, she clicked the TV remote until she found a weather channel. She hit the mute button when she heard her mother's voice.

"JoAnna?"

"Hi, Mom. It's me."

"JoAnna Stedford, where are you?"

"I'm in a little town called Solomon." JoAnna prayed that her mother wouldn't ask the name of her motel. Something named the Swamp Fox Inn would hardly sound pleasing to a worried mother.

"And you are staying at the…?" Maxine paused and waited for JoAnna to fill in the blank.

"Mom, don't be mad. I'd love to tell you I'm at the Hilton or something like that but I'm not. They don't have one here. I'm at the, uh… I'm at the Swamp Fox Inn."

Maxine was silent for a moment. "Very funny, sweetie. Where are you really staying?"

"I'm not joking, Mom. It's called the Swamp Fox Inn. They have real keys for the doors and those old rotary phones like we had in our house when I was little. Can you imagine?" JoAnna hoped a little humor would diffuse the situation.

Maxine exhaled sharply. "Have you been drinking, young lady?"

JoAnna bit her lip and let a moment pass before answering. She was tired and scared, but didn't want her mother to know it so she tried to keep a humorous tone to her voice.

"Yes. Coke and peanuts. And I had a root beer too. But none of the hard stuff."

"What in the world is going on, JoAnna?"

"Promise you won't get mad?"

"I'm already mad. Where are you and what is going on?"

"I'm in Solomon. It's in eastern North Carolina. I'm only a few hours away from the Outer Banks and I'm really staying at a motel called the Swamp Fox Inn. It's the only one in town so I had no choice."

"Why did you stop? Were you too tired to make it all the way to the Outer Banks?"

"No, I'm fine, Mom. I had a little car trouble that's all."

"Car trouble! JoAnna, my car is brand new. And it's a Mercedes. They don't break down until they get very old. What do you mean you had car trouble?" JoAnna cringed as Maxine emphasized the words car and trouble.

"It's not that kind of car trouble, Mom. I have a flat tire. Well, I have two flat tires. That's why I didn't just call for roadside assistance from your insurance company. Both of the front tires are flat. I couldn't just have someone change out a flat tire with the spare."

"Two flat tires? What in the hell happened?" JoAnna was ready for this question. Her prepared answer was a lie, but she knew she had no other choice.

"It was a deer in the road. I couldn't run over it because you how I am when it comes to animals. I saw it at the last minute, swerved to miss it and went off the road. I hit something in the grass and it caused both front tires to blow out. The guy that came with the wrecker looked under the car and said he didn't see any other damage but that I would need to have both tires replaced. He said it didn't look like the tires could be patched so I'll have to get two new ones. He put the car on his wrecker, one of those where the whole car goes up on the back and hauled it to a local garage. He said I could get two new tires there. I'll have to use your credit card. Is that okay?" JoAnna closed her eyes and winced. She knew she was babbling.

"I'm coming out there," Maxine said without answering JoAnna's question about the credit card. "What's the name of the town again?"

JoAnna's frowned. "Mom, please…"

"Don't give me that, JoAnna. I can be there in the morning if I leave now."

"Mom, you don't need to do that. Let me handle this. It's just two tires and nothing else is wrong with the car." She hoped this would enough to placate her mother. She didn't want to tell her that Ray had said it would be hard to find her tires locally, and that they might have to be ordered from out of town. If this turned out to be the case, then she could handle that with her mother when the time came. No need to argue about it now. Right now, she just wanted to talk her mother out of driving to Solomon.

"Mom, I need to handle this on my own. Please. It'll be good for me. They'll get the tires tomorrow and then I'll be on my way. No big deal. And I'll even pay you back for the tires once I start working. I promise."

"JoAnna Stedford, don't talk to me about money. This has nothing to do with money. I don't care about the cost of the tires. I only care about you, young lady. You're out there all by yourself in the middle of nowhere. I've never even heard of, what did you call it? Solomon? Where exactly is that at, anyway?"

"Mom, please. Let me take care of this. I'm okay. Solomon is a little town on the way to the Outer Banks. My motel isn't much, but it's okay. I'm safe. The door is locked and I promise to stay in my room for the rest of the night. Tomorrow I'll go to the garage and get the tires replaced. I'll call you and let you know exactly what's going on." Maxine exhaled into the phone and JoAnna felt like she might be making some headway with her.

"There's a nice little diner close to the motel. I'll get some breakfast there in the morning. Really, everything will be okay."

Maxine paused for a moment. "And you say you're in Solomon, North Carolina at the Swamp Fox Inn. What road is that on?"

"Highway 23. It's a nice little town, Mom. I'll be fine. I'll give you a call first thing in the morning."

"Get yourself some breakfast and then check on the car. Call me after that."

"Then you're okay with this? You're not coming out here?"

"I guess not. You need to stand on your own two feet. I shouldn't always try to be a crutch for you."

JoAnna felt relieved. "Thanks, Mom. I love you. I'll call you tomorrow when I find out about the car."

"I love you too, sweetie."

5

JoAnna felt better after talking to her mother. She walked over to the door and peeked through the edge of the drapes to make sure that Cooper was gone, then scanned what she could see of the parking lot. She opened the door and grabbed the stack of towels, then quickly engaged the deadbolt and privacy bar after shutting the door. She felt a hunger pang and flirted with the idea of ordering a pizza but quickly thought better of it. One stranger knocking on her door tonight was enough. Cooper had set off her alarm bells, and she didn't want to try her luck again with a stranger delivering food. Besides, she doubted Solomon even had a place that would deliver a pizza at this time of night.

The hot shower made her almost feel human again. Once in bed, she clicked through a few channels until she found an old movie. The fear of being alone in a motel room for the first time in her life was not enough to overcome her exhaustion and in a matter of minutes, she was fast asleep.

In the dream, Paul was making slow, passionate love to her on their honeymoon. A thunderstorm lashed against the outside of the rental house, isolating them from the rest of the world. When a crack of thunder shook the house, JoAnna bolted awake and looked quickly around her motel room. She put her hands on her face and tried to calm her nerves, then looked at the digital clock on the nightstand. It was just after midnight.

She collapsed back onto her pillow, turning sideways so that her back was towards the rear wall of the room. Her eyes settled on the edges of the drapes glowing in the darkness. The dream about Paul was always the same, and it always ended with her awakening to find herself alone.

The soft red numbers on the clock floated in the darkness and JoAnna knew she was going to have a hard time falling asleep after her dream. But lying awake and thinking about Paul was what she was supposed to be doing. So much remained unknown to her about his family. Would she be able to find someone in Solomon that could tell her something about them? Her mind drifted back over her and Paul's time together, their dating years, their marriage and then the horrible events that led to his death. Hopefully she hadn't put herself in danger just to find out that no one in town could help her find out more about his family.

She felt the pressure building in her eyes. Here she was, alone in a roadside motel in a strange little town, dreaming of a dead husband that she would never see again. How did it all come to this? What had she done to deserve such a fate? All she had ever wanted to do was to marry Paul and raise a family. Now she was alone. The only person left in the world that cared about her at all was her mother, and even though they had been getting along good lately, she knew this had not always been the case.

JoAnna felt lost in the darkness of the room, like she was stranded deep inside a cave cut off from civilization. She brought her knees up to her chest and curled into a ball while her eyes traced the thin line of light framing the drapes. Suddenly she noticed a shadow pass in front of the window. Adrenaline heated her body when she heard what sounded like a key working in the lock. Someone was outside her door trying to get in and her first instinct was to pull the covers over her head and wait for the end. She wished she had brought a gun, or at the very least a can of pepper spray. Now her worst fear was about to come true.

At that moment, JoAnna decided she was going to fight and she felt a steely resolve gather insider her. She was not going to lie in the bed and wait for the person to unlock the door and break the privacy lock. She knew what would happen then. With more courage than she ever knew she had, she slid out from underneath the covers and moved quickly to the vanity and her makeup bag. Inside of it she had a can of hairspray. It wasn't pepper spray, but it was better than nothing. If the intruder came through the door, she would fill his eyes with the hairspray and then run past him and out into the parking lot and try to flag down a passing car.

JoAnna knew that within seconds the intruder would have both locks unlocked. She moved quickly to the chair next to the TV, grabbed it and then wedged it underneath the doorknob, chiding herself for not remembering to do this before going to bed. Once she had the chair wedged under the doorknob, she grabbed the handle of the deadbolt lock. She could feel the intruder trying to work the lock from the other side.

"Go away!" she yelled. "I've already called the police! Leave me alone!" When she said this, the intruder stopped trying to work the lock. A few seconds passed, and she heard the key being withdrawn. Then she saw a shadow pass again in front of the window.

Despite her threat, JoAnna had completely forgotten to call the police. Did Solomon even have a police department? Surely there was at least a Sheriff. Even though the intruder was no longer outside her door, she held onto the deadbolt lever for another minute or two. She reached down and re-locked the doorknob lock and put her knee against the chair to make sure it was firmly wedged against the door.

A few agonizing minutes passed before she could bring herself to let go of the deadbolt lever and move away from the door. Just as she was about to dial 911 on her cellphone, she saw a flash of light around the edges of the drapes. She peeked through the crack in the drapes and saw a police cruiser pulling up in front of her room. She dressed as quickly as she could, opened the door and waited for the deputy.

"Good evening, Mrs. Stedford. How are you tonight? Is everything okay? My name is Sergeant Hollingsford," the deputy said as he walked up to JoAnna standing in the doorway. She was surprised that he knew her name. How did he know that? Had he already gone to the office and asked Cooper?

"I'm fine now, thank you," JoAnna said. The deputy nodded and then scanned the parking lot looking for anything unusual. Despite her relief at seeing him, JoAnna still felt apprehensive. How did this man know who she was?

"Do you mind me asking how you know my name?" she asked as the deputy returned his eyes to her. He smiled, sensing her nervousness.

"I guess I've known old Ray for years. When I saw him out on the road in his wrecker, I figured something was up and called to him on the radio. He told me all about you and said I should come over here tonight and check up on you. Old Ray is a man of few words but when he speaks it usually counts for something so I knew he had to have a good reason for worrying about you. He told me your name, and all about giving you a tow over to Jared's."

JoAnna exhaled and felt her panic ebb. Ray was worried about her and had asked a deputy to check on her. The world needed more people like that. Joanna smiled at the deputy but he could still see the nervousness in her eyes.

"Is everything okay?"

"Well…" JoAnna stammered. "Well, no it's not. Someone just tried to get in my room. I woke up and saw a shadow go across the window and then the doorknob jiggled. Whoever it was had a key and was trying to unlock my door. I was terrified, so I got out of bed and grabbed my can of hairspray thinking I was going to have to spray it in his eyes if he came through the door."

"You said *he*. How did you know it was a man? Did you see him?"

"Just a guess. I thought someone had seen me go into my room and knew I was in here by myself. And I thought it might have been the night man, too. He made me feel a little uncomfortable when he brought towels to the room earlier tonight. Who else would have a key except him?"

"Cooper? Cooper made you feel uncomfortable?" Hollingsford rubbed his chin and looked over towards the office. "I'll have a little chat with him before I leave. I've known him for a long time and I wouldn't say he's the most stable guy in town, but I don't think he'd hurt you. But then again, you are a young woman staying in a roadside motel all by yourself in a small town. Not the best of situations."

"It's not something I planned, that's for sure. And you don't need to talk to Cooper," JoAnna said quickly. She knew the deputy couldn't stay outside her room all night long and the last thing she wanted was to make Cooper mad because she had reported him to a Sheriff's deputy for something that he might have not done.

"So how long has it been since this person tried to get in your room?" Hollingsford asked as he removed his notepad from his pocket.

"It was right before you drove up."

"Is that so? In that case I'm going to have a look around. I want you to lock your door and don't open it again until I get back."

Ten minutes passed before the deputy returned. When JoAnna heard the knock, she verified him through the peephole and then opened the door.

"Find anyone?"

"No ma'am but I'm going to keep an eye on this motel tonight. I'll pull through the parking lot every half hour or so while I'm on duty. You try to get some sleep and keep your door locked. Don't open it for anyone other than me. Do you understand?"

"I do," replied JoAnna. She tried not to notice the outline of the muscles under Sergeant Hollingsford's shirt. He was tall and strong and she felt good knowing that he was looking out for her. She also knew that he could easily overpower her if he wanted to.

Hollingsford tipped his hat. "Have a good night."

JoAnna closed the door and locked the deadbolt. She watched through the window as Hollingsford climbed back into his cruiser. After sitting for a few minutes to fill out his papers, he drove off across the parking lot. JoAnna watched as the red taillights from the cruiser floated down the road before disappearing in the distance.

6

The remainder of the night passed slowly. After returning to bed JoAnna tried to sleep but the events of the past few hours had upset her so much that all she could manage were short, fitful bouts of sleep. She dosed on and off while staring at the television or the ceiling, and every thirty minutes or so she saw the flash of headlights outside her window. Deputy Hollingsford was checking up on her just as he had promised. Despite this, she was still unable to get much sleep and was relieved when she finally saw the pink glow of dawn illuminating the edges of the drapes.

Once the sun was up, JoAnna got out of bed and double checked the locks on the door. She peeked out of the window at the gravel parking lot and saw that it was still empty, except for Cooper's old beat-up car. She looked across the lot at the diner and felt her stomach rumble.

After her shower, JoAnna dressed and packed up her bags. She thought about Cooper's offer of the complimentary continental breakfast, but she wanted more than just donuts. Besides, he was the last person she wanted to see right now since he was obviously the one that had tried to get in her room last night.

JoAnna slipped the room key into her pocket and closed the door behind her. The air smelled of smoke and pine trees and she could see the swamp canal behind the motel covered with a blanket of hazy fog. As she walked across the parking lot, she noticed a large flatbed wrecker parked beside the diner.

Barely a head turned when she walked into the diner. Several patrons were sitting at the bar with their backs to the door and only one of them turned around to look at her. After examining her for a few seconds, he smiled curtly and returned to eating his breakfast. Ray sat in a corner booth and when he saw JoAnna he gave her a tip of his ball cap before taking a sip of his coffee.

"Mr. Greenfield?" JoAnna said as she approached Ray. He swallowed his sip of coffee and then sat his cup on the table.

"Everybody in town calls me Ray."

She smiled. "I'd just like to thank you for asking that deputy to check on me last night. It really helped. I had a scare, and he showed up at almost the perfect time. It made me feel a lot better."

Ray looked at JoAnna with a puzzled look on his face, then scanned the empty tables in the diner.

"You're welcome to sit by yourself but if you'd like to have a seat with me it's okay."

"Don't mind if I do," JoAnna said just as a server appeared with a pot of coffee.

"Well, hello there. I'm Lydia." She examined JoAnna and then her curiosity got the best of her. "Are you new in town?" Ray looked up at Lydia and then slid his coffee cup towards her. She took the hint and promptly topped it off for him.

"Oh, I'm just passing through. I had car trouble last night. Ray here helped me out and gave me a tow. I should be leaving sometime today." JoAnna turned the coffee mug in front of her right side up so that Lydia could fill it with coffee.

JoAnna ordered bacon and eggs over easy with a side of hash browns and wheat toast. Ray raised an eyebrow as he listened to her order. Lydia smiled, tore the order slip from her pad and disappeared.

"Thanks again for speaking to the deputy," JoAnna said. Ray raised his eyebrows again as he watched her pour sugar and creamer into her already full cup. When finished she could barely stir the coffee without causing it to spill over the rim.

"They never give you enough room for the good stuff that goes with the coffee," she said as she picked up her cup and took a sip out of it. Ray smiled and looked down into his cup of black coffee.

"I guess not, missy. Do you like coffee with that sugar and cream?"

JoAnna smiled at Ray. "I guess it's about as sweet as a coffee milkshake. My daddy used to make it like this for me when I was a little girl. He called it white coffee because he put so much cream in it that it turned the coffee white. I've just never been able to drink it any other way." She smiled and took a long sip. "Mmmm, that's just perfect."

The look in Ray's eyes caught her off guard. She had seen it before when he had helped her with her car the night before, but it had been dark and she hadn't been able to see his eyes all that well under the bib of his cap. Now in the light of the diner she could see his eyes clearly. They looked dark and distance, almost lifeless. Ray seemed like a nice man, but his eyes conveyed a different message than his outward appearance. She didn't know if it was something she should fear, or if it was just her imagination. But Ray's eyes seemed to be telling her something, and if she didn't know better, she thought they were warning her. Unnerved, she looked back down into her coffee just as Lydia showed up with her breakfast.

"I'm starving," she said to Ray as she began to salt and pepper her eggs. When she looked up at Ray again, she noticed his eyes had grown sad. She didn't know what to make of it so she turned her attention to her food.

"This looks delicious," JoAnna said as she took a bite of her eggs. After a few more bites she dabbed her chin with her napkin and thanked Ray again for talking to the deputy.

"Missy, I don't know why you keep thanking me for that. I didn't talk to a deputy last night." JoAnna watched his dark eyes drift from her back down to his coffee.

She frowned as her fork stopped in midair. "But the deputy said he talked to you. His name was Hollingsford." She tried to ignore the alarm bells going off in her head. "He knew my name, and all about my car." To hide her nervousness, JoAnna put her fork down and took a long pull from her coffee cup.

"I'm sayin' I didn't talk to a deputy." Ray's eyes left JoAnna, and he looked past her through the large front window of the diner. He spied a Sheriff's department cruiser as it rolled past the diner, then his eyes settled back on JoAnna.

"I'm sorry missy. I guess I'm just gettin' old." Ray looked over to a spot on the other side of the diner. "I don't know how much longer this will last." He took a long sip and then looked at her again, his eyes as black as the swamp water in the canal.

JoAnna crinkled her brow. "I... I don't understand."

Ray sighed. "I'm sayin' that now that I think of it, I guess I did get on the radio last night. The Sheriff around these parts likes for me to report any tow that I make, especially if the car was in an accident. It seems now I remember calling in and talking to a deputy on my squawk box. That must be the one that came by to see you."

JoAnna felt a wave of relief rush through her body. Ray had talked to the deputy after all. Maybe he was just old and had a hard time remembering things. That was certainly normal. But what did he mean when he said that he didn't know how much longer this would last? She didn't want to ask, so she returned to eating her breakfast.

After a few more bites of food, she decided to change the subject from the deputy to something else. She thought about Paul's story on their honeymoon night when he stopped at the gas station to get a soda. Looking back on that night and thinking about what Paul had said, she was sure Ray was the old man from Paul's story.

"You may not believe this Ray, but I think you met my husband once. It was a little over a year ago. We were on our honeymoon and came through here on our way to the Outer Banks. I was asleep in the car and he stopped at your gas station to get a soda. I slept through the whole thing but he told me later that a man with a big dog at an old gas station gave him a real scare."

Ray looked at JoAnna and she could see in his dark eyes that he was searching his memory.

"I don't remember, missy. I'm old and it's hard to remember what I did yesterday, much less a year ago. Don't know how much longer this will last." Ray took a long drink of his coffee. "But I don't doubt it. I'm usually up late at night checkin' on things. And I did have a dog, but he's gone now. Died a few months ago. I miss him. He looked out for me and my wife."

"Your wife?" JoAnna said as she covered her hash browns with ketchup. "Have you been married long?" She hoped her question wasn't too personal.

Ray nodded his head. "Over fifty years. We never had children, so it was just us and the dog. He really watched over us but a truck hit him out on the highway so he's gone now." Ray returned his attention to his coffee cup. "Wife's gone too."

JoAnna felt her heart go out to the old man. She wiped her mouth with a napkin and looked at Ray, not knowing what else to say. "That's so sad. I'm so sorry, Ray. But I know how it feels to be alone. My husband died a little over a year ago. That's why I'm out here on the road all by myself. I'm having a hard time dealing with him being gone and I, well I know this will sound stupid, but I'm out here on the road retracing our honeymoon trip. You know, just for the memories. My mom keeps telling me I should move on, and I'm trying to, but it's easier said than done. It's hard to be a woman and be alone with no one in the world. I'm lucky, I guess, because I still have my mother so I'm not completely alone. But I miss my husband terribly."

Ray's dark eyes settled on JoAnna. He could tell that grief was weighing heavily on her. Just as he had helped her the night before, he decided it was time to try to help her again.

"You seem sad, missy. I'm sayin' that you might like to visit Madam Valentine. I told you about her last night. The woman knows things. She might be able to help you move on. Most people don't believe in all that palm reading hocus pocus, but I'm sayin' she knows things. She can help you with your grief."

JoAnna looked at Ray and tried to smile. She didn't want to offend him but she didn't believe in psychics and had no intention of starting now. But Ray had been so helpful to her, and he was an old man with problems of his own, so she decided to go along with his suggestion.

"Well, you know what? I'll probably get bored today while they work on my car so maybe I'll walk to her house. It's not that far from the garage."

"Tell her Ray sent you. I'm sayin' she'll give you a good price."

JoAnna smiled. "Will do."

She finished off her hash browns and then buttered the rest of her toast. After applying a little grape jelly, she finished off both pieces. When she noticed Ray watching her eat, she tried to hide her embarrassment.

"I'm sorry, Ray. My husband always gave me the same look. He always called me a chow hound, whatever that means."

Ray smiled, then his dark eyes drifted across the diner. Only a few patrons were sitting at the bar and the rest of the booths were empty.

"Do you mind if I ask you another question, Ray?"

Ray turned his head. "Shoot, missy."

"Do you know anyone in town named Stedford?"

Ray searched his memory. "That name sounds familiar, but I can't remember why. Like I said, I'm getting old and my memory ain't what it used to be."

"I understand," JoAnna said as she took one last sip of her coffee.

"If you're finished, I'll give you a ride down to Jared's so you can check on your car. I'm sayin' it ain't far, but I can still give you a ride. And maybe I can have a chat with Jared to keep him honest about your tires. He has a habit of overcharging people from out of town."

JoAnna reached for her purse. "I would really appreciate that. Garages make me nervous. I don't know much about cars except how to put gas in them. Let me get your breakfast for you as a show of my gratitude." JoAnna produced a few dollar bills from her purse and slid them under her plate for a tip, then grabbed both tickets that Lydia had left on the table after topping off their coffee cups.

"Missy, that's not…"

JoAnna held up her hand. "Mr. Greenfield, I insist. You gave me a free tow last night and you're helping me again this morning. It's the least I can do."

"Everybody in town calls me Ray."

"I know. And if you want me to keep calling you Ray then you'll let me buy your breakfast." JoAnna gave Ray a crooked smile as she slid out of her seat.

"Suit yourself, missy. Much obliged."

JoAnna walked to the cash register and handed both tickets to Lydia while Ray waited on her by the door. Once outside they climbed into his wrecker and began the short drive to Jared's garage.

Out of the corner of her eye, JoAnna spied Madam Valentine's house sitting by the side of the road. As Ray turned down the street towards Jared's garage, she watched through the side window and thought to herself that she maybe she should take the old man's advice and go see the woman. If nothing else, it would be an interesting story to tell her mother.

7

Jared watched as the wrecker pulled into his parking lot. He knew who the lady was riding with Ray before she even came into his office. He reached up and rubbed his salt and pepper goatee when they walked through the door.

"Morning Ray. Good morning to you too, ma'am."

"Good morning. I'm JoAnna Stedford."

Jared nodded. "I've already looked at your Mercedes, Miss Stedford. It's gonna take two new tires and a front-end alignment. Sorry, but I don't stock tires like that in my shop. If I did, they'd dry rot on the rack before I could sell them."

JoAnna looked at Ray and then back at Jared. "How long will it take to get them?"

Jared wiped his hands with his rag. "I know a guy in Greenville and he said he could have them to me by tomorrow. But he wants me to buy the whole set. All four of them. I told him I only need two, but well, you know. He's funny like that." Jared smiled and then looked over at Ray, who cleared his throat and narrowed his eyes.

"Well…" Jared stammered. "Maybe I can call him back and tell him I only need two tires. He owes me a favor, anyway. Last week I sent him a master cylinder for a '69 Camaro. He was looking all over the place for one." Ray nodded his approval when Jared said this.

Jared returned Ray's stare with a look that showed his irritation with the old man. But Ray had been bringing him business for decades and he knew better than to upset him. For some reason Ray had taken a shine to the young woman driving the Mercedes and was not going to let her be the victim of the usual shakedown he administered to people from out of town.

JoAnna frowned. "Tomorrow? Can he get them here today? I was hoping to leave this afternoon." She turned and looked at Ray.

"I'm sorry, Miss Stedford, but that's the best I can do."

Frustrated, JoAnna said, "Okay then. But can you please try to get done as fast as you can?"

"We aim to please, ma'am. I'll put Pike on it. He's my best mechanic, and he does all the front-end work." Jared walked to the repair bay door and called for Pike. When he walked into the office a few minutes later, he seemed shy and didn't want to make eye contact with them.

"Pike, you will handle Miss Stedford's Mercedes. The tires will be here tomorrow. You'll have to align the front end too. And be sure to take off your damn belt buckle. I don't want you leaning over the fender and scratching that pretty red paint."

"Yes sir," replied Pike. He tilted his head back slightly and peered at JoAnna from underneath the bib on his hat. It was then that she noticed his eyes. They were as black and emotionless as Ray's. She stared at Pike for a few seconds, then looked at Jared.

"Pike here will do you right, Miss Stedford. And you asked me about the cost. It will probably be about four hundred and fifty dollars give or take. I won't be able to give you an exact number until I see how long it takes Pike to do the work. Labor is by the hour."

JoAnna exhaled again. She felt tension claw at her stomach. Her mother was going to have a fit and she was already dreading the phone call.

"Well, I guess I don't have a lot of options." She turned to Ray, and he looked at her with his brooding eyes. He nodded his head slightly, signaling that it was about the best she was going get considering her situation.

"If you'll give me your cell number, I'll call and keep you updated. You're probably staying at the Swamp Fox Inn, right?" Jared knew there was only one motel in town.

"I did last night. I guess I'll be there tonight since there is nowhere else to stay." When Pike heard this, his charcoal-colored eyes widened. He looked at JoAnna again and then turned and walked back into the repair bay. A few seconds later, the ratta-tat-tat of his impact wrench resumed. Jared shook his head and then turned back to JoAnna and Ray.

"No need to sit around here in this office reading my old

magazines all day, Miss Stedford. There's not much in town, but anything is better than sitting here in my shop. We've got a diner and their coffee is pretty good."

"I know," replied JoAnna. "I had breakfast there. Ray and I that is."

"And we got us a real live palm reader here in town too. I'm sure you saw her house on the way in."

"I'll find something to do." JoAnna tried not to roll her eyes. *What is it with these people and the palm reader?* "And I'll call you later today to check on your progress," she said before she turned and walked to the door of the office. Ray nodded at Jared and followed JoAnna into the parking lot. They climbed into the wrecker and drove off in the direction of the motel.

JoAnna asked Ray to take her back to the diner. She told him she would have another cup of coffee and then think about what she was going to do for the rest of the day. He dropped her at the diner and told her if she needed anything to give him a call. She was glad Ray was dropping her off and not coming into the diner. It was true that she wanted a cup of coffee, but she also knew she was going to have to call her mother. And that was a conversation that she didn't want to have in front of Ray.

"Coffee?" asked Lydia once JoAnna took a seat.

"That would be great." JoAnna smiled and turned her cup right side up and slid it towards the edge of the table.

After getting the coffee just right with cream and sugar, JoAnna pulled out her cellphone and dialed her mother's home number. There was no answer. She frowned at her phone and hit the cancel button, then dialed her mother's cell number. Again, there was no answer. Suddenly she felt a pang of relief at the idea of not having to tell her mother about the tires, but she also felt worried at the same time. It was odd for her mother to not answer her cell.

Lydia returned after a few minutes and removed her order pad from her pocket.

"Aren't you the girl that came in this morning with Raymond?" JoAnna grinned.

"Yep. And he said everybody in town calls him Ray." JoAnna canceled her call and dropped her phone in her purse. Lydia rolled her eyes and smiled.

"I know, I know. I call him Raymond sometimes just to get a rise out of him. You're staying at the Swamp Fox?" Lydia looked over her shoulder and then back at JoAnna. "Watch out for Cooper. He's a creep. They fired him from the mill years ago for coming in drunk and he's been the night man at the motel ever since. His cousin is the owner. That's the only way he got the job."

JoAnna looked at Lydia and tried to hide her astonishment. This certainly helped her understand Cooper and the incident last night. He had probably gotten drunk before coming to her door.

"You know, I think I'll wait on lunch. I had that big breakfast with Ray this morning but the coffee is good. You can keep that coming." JoAnna closed the menu and tried to stick it back in the rack holding the salt and pepper shakers.

"Do you like the Swamp Fox?" Lydia said as JoAnna fumbled with the menu trying to get it to stand up in the rack.

"Well, not really. I mean, it's okay, but someone tried to get in my room last night and it scared the bejesus out of me." She gave up on the menu and turned her attention to Lydia.

Lydia huffed. "Cooper… Like I said, he's the town creep."

JoAnna took a sip of her coffee. "I can believe it."

Lydia felt sympathy well up inside her. Here was a young, pretty girl sitting in a diner in a lonely town in the middle of nowhere. She was staying at a ratty motel and had already had her wits scared out of her, and to top it all off she had car trouble. Lydia considered all of this and then slid into the seat across from JoAnna.

"The boss won't mind," she said with a wink. JoAnna smiled weakly, unsure of what to say.

"Listen, I can tell you're really scared. I mean, if I had to sleep just a few doors down from Cooper and his whiskey bottle I'd be scared too. No one in town likes him."

JoAnna looked across the table at Lydia and felt at ease. It was nice to have another girl close to her age to talk to. She decided to share some of her grief.

"My husband is gone. He died not too long ago." JoAnna winced as the words left her mouth.

Compassion filled Lydia's eyes. "It's gonna be okay," she said as she patted JoAnna's hand.

"I know. It's just hard. I feel so alone. I miss him so much."

Lydia nodded. "You know, my husband loved his motorcycle." JoAnna tilted her head when Lydia said this. She didn't understand what it had to do with anything.

"Yep. He loved that damned motorcycle. Just a few months ago he was riding home from Poplar, a little town just north of here. He'd gone hunting with some friends of his and was riding home in the rain. I tried to tell that damn fool…" Lydia reached over to the napkin dispenser on the table, yanked out a napkin and wiped her eyes. "I tried to tell that damn fool not to ride so fast. So pigheaded… These old country roads, lined with trees and swamps… I always tried to tell him not to ride so fast, and not to ride in the rain. He hit a curve going too fast and went right off the road and into a pine tree. No one much travels that road, so his body laid out there all night long. When I woke up in the morning and he wasn't home, I got in my car and drove towards Poplar. I saw the bike. He was dead when I found him."

JoAnna's mouth dropped open. "I'm… I'm so sorry," she said as Lydia wiped her eyes again with the napkin. "Looks like we've got something in common."

A weak smile crossed Lydia's face. "Look at us. We're just a mess. Sitting here crying like this."

"I know…" JoAnna said. "But it's really hard. And for me it's been a year. I can imagine how hard it is for you. You must still be grieving. I was so bad off right after my husband's death that I needed therapy. It lasted for a year and I thought I'd never get over it." JoAnna knew she wasn't being completely truthful with Lydia. Even though it had been a year, her grief was just as fresh as it had been on the day she had buried Paul.

Lydia looked at JoAnna as her eyes clouded over. "I'm doing better. In fact, everything is going to be okay. I just know it. Everything's going to be okay." Lydia turned her head and stared out of the side window. After a few moments, she turned back and looked at JoAnna.

"Hey, I've got an idea. If you've got to stay another night until old Jared gets done with your car, why don't you just stay with me? I've got a pretty comfortable couch and I can promise you that Cooper won't bother you at my place." Lydia patted JoAnna on the hand. "What do you say? No more scary nights at the Swamp Fox? I've got a bottle of whiskey too. It's homemade. We can get snockered."

JoAnna beamed as she considered Lydia's offer. "I'd love to. I was really dreading another night at that motel. Honestly, I was considering just finding a bridge to sleep under if you want to know the truth. Anything would be better than Cooper trying to get in my room."

"Well you don't have to sleep under a bridge. You can sleep on my couch. After all, we're kindred spirits seeing as how we've both lost our husbands."

"It's a deal," replied JoAnna.

"I get off in a few hours. You can hang out here if you want to, and as long as you keep buying coffee and maybe some lunch or something the owner won't care if you sit here all afternoon."

"I'll get my bags from my motel room," JoAnna replied. "I guess I can bring them back here so I don't look like a vagrant walking around town with a duffel bag over my shoulder."

Lydia tapped her chin with her pen. "Just go get your stuff and we'll stick it in my car."

"Okay," JoAnna said. "That's sounds like a good idea. Are you sure you don't mind?"

"Nope." Lydia tapped her chin one more time with her pen. "Like I said, you and I are kindred spirits. I don't mind at all. I don't usually invite strangers to spend the night with me but you don't look like the type that would chop me up with a hatchet in my sleep so I think I can take a chance just this once."

JoAnna chuckled and then looked out the window. "By the way, what's the deal with the palm reader? Both Ray and Jared suggested I go see her. Do you believe in that stuff?"

Lydia's eyes darkened. "She could help you. They say that palm reading stuff is all a bunch of baloney, but I've gone to her before. I went right after, well, you know. Right after it happened. She helped me."

"Really? You went to see her?"

"Yep, and it did me a lot of good. The woman has a gift. It would be something for you to do to kill some time. Like I said, I don't get off for a few hours. You can leave your stuff in my car and walk to her house. It's not far."

JoAnna took another sip of her coffee. "Well, it's not like I have anything better to do. I guess it would beat sitting here drinking coffee all afternoon even though it's good coffee. I was just thinking the other day that I could use a good palm reading. Wait until I tell my mother. I'll never hear the end of it. Speaking of that, I need to give her another call."

"I'll leave you alone so you can call her. When you get your stuff, just come in and get me and we'll put it in my car."

"Okay," JoAnna said as she dialed her mother's number. She put the phone to her ear just as a burly truck driver walked into the diner and sat down at the counter.

8

Madam Valentine's house was small and well-kept cottage with a manicured yard. Ornate wooden molding trimmed the edges of the roof and colorful plants sat along the edge of the front porch. JoAnna grinned as she walked up the steps to the front door. She turned the tarnished copper doorknob and stepped into the small front parlor of the home and when she didn't see anyone inside, she wondered if Madam Valentine was open for business. There had been no sign on the door saying otherwise.

"Hello?" JoAnna examined the walls while she waited for a response. Picture frames containing very old photographs hung intermittently around the room against pastel-colored wallpaper. Most of the photographs were old and grainy and looked like they had been taken right after the invention of the camera. Hazy daylight filtered through the windows providing the only light in the room. Just as she was about to walk over to examine one of the larger portraits, a woman appeared in the doorway that led to the rear of the house.

"JoAnna! It's so nice to see you." Cassandra Valentine beamed as she stepped into the parlor.

Okay, Ray could have told her I was coming. Lydia could have told her too, JoAnna thought to herself when Madam Valentine called her by name. She tried to hide her surprise and instead decided to be coy about it.

"I guess my name is all over town by now. I'm the out-of-towner that almost skidded into the swamp canal in my car. I'm the JoAnna Stedford that I'm sure everyone is talking about. It's nice to meet you. You must be Madam Valentine. I've heard an awful lot about you." She took a few steps and extended her hand. Madam Valentine reached out with both of her hands and squeezed JoAnna's hand instead of shaking it.

"Yes, I'm Cassandra Valentine. You can all me Cassandra or Madam Valentine. Believe it or not, it's actually my real family name and not some sort of phony stage name I picked just to look good on a sign. I was named after my great great-grandmother." Madam Valentine beamed with pride. "What can I do for you?"

The woman looked exactly opposite of what JoAnna expected. Dressed in jeans and a colorful long sleeve shirt with the cuffs rolled up to the middle of her forearms, Madam Valentine looked like she had just stepped out of the pages of a homemaking magazine. Her long black hair spilled onto her shoulders, with bangs that hovered just above her green eyes. She looked nothing like what JoAnna thought a psychic should look like.

"Well, I'm waiting on my car to be repaired. You've probably heard. I just thought I would come down and get a palm reading. I should tell you, I'm really not a believer but they have to order stuff for my car, tires and so forth, so I have some free time today and tomorrow. Everyone I've met seems to speak highly of you, especially Ray, so I thought I'd give it a try."

"Give it a try?" Madam Valentine raised an eyebrow as a crooked grin shot across her face.

"You know, let you read my palm." JoAnna hoped she had not offended the woman.

"Well let's get started then. My fee is only twenty dollars since you're friends with Ray. If you'll come this way, we'll get down to business."

They walked down the short hallway until they came to another room. In place of a door, strings of colorful beads hung across the doorway. A small round table sat in the middle of the room surrounded by several antique chairs with plush red velvet cushions. A sheet of hammered copper covered the top of the table and in one corner of the room stood a headless mannequin adorned with flamboyant clothes. Madam Valentine motioned for JoAnna to sit in one of the chairs.

"Before we begin, would you like something to drink? Sweet tea? Water? Wine, perhaps?"

"No thank you," replied JoAnna. She watched as Madam

Valentine walked to the corner of the room and turned on a small lamp sitting on top of a bookcase.

"I have to be honest with you," JoAnna said as Madam Valentine sat down across from her. "Please don't be offended, but I was expecting someone dressed up like a Genie. You really don't look like a psychic, not that I really know what an average psychic is supposed to look like." She chuckled and looked down at the burnished copper on the tabletop. When she looked up, Madam Valentine eyes were aglow with humor.

"You mean clothes that look more like those." She nodded towards the mannequin. "In my business you will find that the more flamboyant the psychic, the more likely it is that she, or he, is a fake. I have no need to dress up like a Genie as you put it. Nor do I need one of those crystal balls like you see at the county fair. All I need are your hands and for you to have an open mind."

JoAnna frowned and started to apologize, but Madam Valentine interrupted her.

"But I know what you're saying, JoAnna. Take that mannequin over there. Those clothes on it, they belonged to my grandmother. She was in the business too. In fact, this house was her home. Back then Solomon was much bigger than it is now and she made a good living telling fortunes. Trouble is she didn't really have the power. Not like I do, anyway. And she wore flamboyant clothes to make up for it and did a lot of snooping around to find out things about people so she could then pretend to tell them their fortune. She was more into showmanship than anything else. I kept one of her outfits after she died and I put it on that mannequin over there to remind me of her. I loved her dearly." Madam Valentine then extended her hands across the table. "Shall we begin?"

JoAnna paused and then extended her right hand. Madam Valentine smiled understandingly. "I need both of your hands, dear." JoAnna hesitated and then extended her other hand. She felt the cool copper of the tabletop and wondered to herself how many people before her had placed their hands on the old table hoping for a glimpse of the future.

Madam Valentine laid her hands on top of JoAnna's so that their palms were touching. She grinned when she saw the look on JoAnna's face.

"You probably thought I was going to trace your heart line and then tell you that I see a winning lottery ticket and a dark, handsome man in your future."

"Isn't that how it's done?"

"Not with me." Madam Valentine pressed her palms against JoAnna's. "They say that the eyes are the windows of the soul. This is true, but we use our hands to touch the things in our lives that are dear to us, like our loved ones. And the hands remember. They tell me everything, like where a person has been, who they have loved, who they have hated, what has brought them joy or sorrow. And they can tell me where what lies ahead. Now if you'll close your eyes, we'll begin."

JoAnna closed her eyes and after a few seconds her arms started to tingle. She felt Madam Valentine's hands on hers, warm and comforting, and her mind began to drift as the tingling in her arms rose past her elbows. Madam Valentine took a deep breath and exhaled as her hands pressed down on JoAnna's.

"So much grief…" A frown clouded her face. "How long has it been? How long has he been gone?"

JoAnna opened her eyes and looked at Madam Valentine, whose jade-colored eyes seemed to shimmer in the dim light of the room.

"Gone?" JoAnna paused. "He's been gone for a little over a year." JoAnna knew she had told Lydia about Paul's death. This was proof that word travels fast in a small town.

"So much grief… You are finding it hard to go on without him."

"Yes," replied JoAnna, knowing this revelation was hardly proof of Madam Valentine's psychic ability. What wife wouldn't miss her dead husband?

"Yes, I miss him and it is hard to be without him." JoAnna figured she would go along with the routine. She vowed to tell Lydia that she was onto their little joke once she got back to the diner.

Suddenly Madam Valentine's face darkened. Fear blazed in her eyes as she took both of JoAnna's hands into hers and squeezed them slightly. *Theatrics*, JoAnna thought to herself as she watched. A few moments passed and then Madam Valentine looked JoAnna in the eyes and spoke in a soft whisper. "He took his own life."

JoAnna drew in a breath. She knew that she hadn't told Lydia, or anyone else in Solomon that Paul had killed himself. Panic, warm and toxic, shot through her veins.

Madam Valentine continued. "Just as his father before him."

JoAnna felt a shiver and tried to pull her hands away but Madam Valentine only tightened her grip.

"Do not break our bond, JoAnna. If you want my help, you must not break our bond."

JoAnna tried to calm herself as the battle raged inside her. She wanted to hear more, but at the same time was fearful of what would come next.

Madam Valentine closed her eyes drifted away for a moment. "And I see a child…"

A tear rolled down JoAnna's cheek. She tried once again to pull her hands away from Madam Valentine, but this time she felt her resolve weaken.

"The child is gone too. You have lost a child, JoAnna."

JoAnna's hands went limp and she began to sob. She knew there was no way this woman could know these things about her unless she really had the power. When she looked at Madam Valentine's face, she could see the fear and apprehension. "What… What is it?" she asked, terrified at what she might hear.

"You are being followed, JoAnna. He is restless and he will not stop until he gets what he wants. His ghost walks among us because he is not finished in this world."

"Who?" JoAnna's chin quivered. She already knew the answer to her question.

"The father. I see him. He feeds on your grief."

JoAnna tilted her face and wiped the tears from her eyes using her shirtsleeve. She knew that Lydia was right. This woman could help her. She decided to try to get answers from Madam Valentine about the things going on in her life, things that she was not able to talk to anyone else about.

"Yes. I have seen him. It's because of him that I'm stranded in this town. I saw him in the road and it caused me to wreck my car." Then she asked the one question that she most wanted an answer to.

"Why? Why is he here?"

Madam Valentine frowned. "I don't know, JoAnna. I cannot see it. I'm sorry. But I can see the grief that is consuming you." Madam Valentine opened her eyes and looked at JoAnna. "You must move on. Time will dull the sharp edge of the grief. You must leave it behind you. You're young and your whole life is ahead of you, JoAnna."

"I can't," JoAnna said as the tears rolled down her cheeks. "I will never get over him. He was my life. I never want anyone else."

Madam Valentine squeezed JoAnna's hands again. Frustration flashed in her green eyes.

"He's gone, JoAnna. You must move on. You must…"

"I said I can't! JoAnna snapped. I told my mother I could. I told her if I came on this trip it would help me to move on, but it was a lie. I will never get over Paul. I don't want to get over him." JoAnna paused and collected herself. "There is no other man for me."

"JoAnna…"

"No! I said no!" JoAnna's emotions were a kaleidoscope of heartache, anger and fear. She jerked her hands out of Madam Valentine's grasp and leaned back in the velvet chair, then put her face in her hands. After a few minutes of silence, she composed herself.

"I want to help you, JoAnna. Many people come to me to try to contact their lost loved ones so I've seen my share of grieving wives and husbands. With a little help they are always able to move on. But sometimes just seeing their loved ones through me is not enough for them. They need more. I think you are that kind of person. And you remind me of a young woman that came to see me several months ago. She too said she could not move on. Her grief was on the level of yours and I was able to offer her another route."

JoAnna wiped her eyes and wondered if the young woman was Lydia. After all, Lydia had admitted that she had visited Madam Valentine and that the visit had helped her. She reached for a tissue and dabbed her eyes.

"JoAnna, sometimes I am not able to help a person. There are times when I just don't have the power to do that." Madam Valentine paused and then clasped her hands together to try to hide her nervousness. She knew what JoAnna needed, what the only solution was for her, but she was reluctant to offer it to her. But as she looked at JoAnna sitting across from her at the table, her cheeks wet with tears of grief and her heart crying out for her dead husband, she knew that she had to tell her that there was another person in town that might be able to help her deal with her grief.

"JoAnna, there is another woman in Solomon that may be able to help you. She offers, well… she offers something a little different from what I offer. Perhaps you should go see her. Her name is Pearl.

Isabelle Pearl. She lives in an old house outside of town."

"What does she offer?" asked JoAnna as she wiped the last of the tears from her eyes. "Is she a psychic too?"

"I'd rather not say. She is… different. I cannot offer you what she can. I cannot take you where she can take you. But you must remember JoAnna that everything comes with a price. Please remember that if you talk to her. My price is simple. It is twenty dollars for a reading, but Isabelle Pearl will not help you for money. Her fee is something different and she will discuss it with you. But I can tell you that her price is different for every client."

"Madam…"

"Please call me Cassandra."

JoAnna smiled. "Cassandra," she said as she sniffled into her tissue. "I'm not sure I understand."

"I really can't say more, JoAnna. If you feel, as you said, that you will never get over your husband and that you can't go on without him, then I suggest you go see Isabelle Pearl. She is the next step for you."

JoAnna looked so forlorn sitting in the small velvet-covered chair that Madam Valentine felt her heart break for her. *So much life ahead of her,* she thought to herself.

"But I can tell you that if you let grief consume your life, the ghost of your husband's father will haunt you for the rest of your days. End the grief, and you will end his presence in your life. That is all I can offer you regarding him. As for your husband, his soul is a tortured and restless presence. He regrets what he did and wants to be with you. I could see him during our reading. But I cannot take you any further. The only person that can do that is Isabelle Pearl."

JoAnna exhaled sharply and looked at Madam Valentine. "Isabelle Pearl? I don't know what she could do for me. I mean, you've helped me a lot. I don't know what the next step could be. My husband is gone and is never coming back. I guess I'm just going to spend the rest of my life alone thinking about him."

"That would be a sad way to spend your life, JoAnna. If that is your plan, I encourage you to seek out Isabelle Pearl."

"Okay. I mean, I guess so." JoAnna wiped her nose again with her tissue. "I'll ask Lydia about her. I'm sure she'll know how to get to her house."

"I can say most assuredly that she does, JoAnna." Both women rose from the table and walked to the front of the house. JoAnna dug into her purse and then handed Madam Valentine a twenty-dollar bill.

"Remember, JoAnna. This is my fee. Nothing is ever free in this world. You know this, and so does Isabelle Pearl."

JoAnna felt her scalp tingle. "I'll remember that, Cassandra. Thank you again. You certainly have helped me. I guess you're the real thing. I'm sorry I doubted you."

"It's my gift, JoAnna. And to think, I can do it without dressing up like a Genie."

JoAnna walked out of the house into the bright sunlight. For the first time in a long time, she had hope even though she wasn't sure what it meant. As she walked down the sidewalk towards the diner, she thought about taking Lydia up on her offer to have a little whiskey tonight. Maybe after a few drinks, Lydia would open up about her visit to this Isabelle Pearl woman.

9

JoAnna sat in the passenger's seat of Lydia's car watching the buildings glide by as they drove down the main road through Solomon. They passed the *Astro-wash* car wash and JoAnna noticed that all the stalls were empty.

"The town's dying," Lydia said when she noticed JoAnna looking at the empty car wash. "Used to be more people here, but the mill has been winding down for years now. Lots of folks have moved away."

"Looks like it," JoAnna said, as she watched other buildings go by. Most were boarded up but some were still open for business.

"That's what we're going to do." Lydia then corrected herself. "I mean, that's what we were going to do, anyway. You know, before the accident. We talked about moving far away where no one would know us. Get us a fresh start in a new town. There's nothing here but swamps and that old finishing mill, and I'd rather be a prostitute than go to work in that place."

They turned off the main road onto a side street. JoAnna watched as they drove by a lonely Post Office with only one car in the parking lot. After a few more turns they arrived at Lydia's trailer. JoAnna made it a point not to frown when they pulled up in the gravel driveway. When she brought the car to a stop, Lydia looked wistfully at the front porch. "I know it's not much, but it's home. See that porch? My husband built it. The damn fool…" JoAnna looked at the ungainly porch attached to the front of the trailer.

"It looks nice. He must have been a real handyman."

"Yeah, he was. He wanted one of those above-ground pools too, but we couldn't afford it." Lydia drifted away for a few moments.

"He promised he was going to buy me a house one day. Like I said, we wanted to move away to a new town. Get good jobs and buy a house. But then…"

JoAnna reached over and patted Lydia's hand. "It's going to be okay. You said so yourself."

A smile returned to Lydia's face. "I did. And you know what? I was right." She looked back at the trailer and then at JoAnna.

"How about I show you my humble abode? Somewhere in there is a bottle of whiskey with our names on it. Let's go see if we can find it." Lydia gave JoAnna a wink as she shut off the engine.

The inside of the trailer was modest. JoAnna remembered how Paul had once chided her for not knowing how less fortunate people lived. They had been on their way to Charleston and had stopped at a gas station that was in the middle of what Paul had told her was a mill village. She had made a few comments about how small the houses were and how they had all looked alike. She had asked Paul how people lived in such small houses and he had scolded her for not understanding that some people had it much rougher than others. JoAnna now found herself standing in the small living room of just that type of person.

Lydia had a small couch that looked very comfortable. A table made from an empty cable spool sat in front of the couch. Lydia noticed JoAnna looking at it.

"My husband got that from the power company. He had a friend that works as a lineman. The damn fool… I complained about it but I finally agreed to let him bring it in to use as a table. Now it makes me think about him. I wouldn't trade it for a bar of gold."

A small TV sat on a stand in the middle of the living room wall. Another chair sat next to the cable spool that appeared to be about as old as the couch. JoAnna looked across the room at the kitchen and saw that it was small but very clean, with no dirty dishes in the sink. Despite the age of the furnishings, Lydia was obviously a good housekeeper who took pride her home.

Lydia dropped her purse on the kitchen counter. "Make yourself at home, girlfriend."

"You can call me Jo, that's sort of my nickname." JoAnna walked into the middle of the small living room. "My husband called me that a lot. He was a damn fool too." She was starting to feel very comfortable with Lydia and realized that despite their different backgrounds they had a lot in common.

"Jo it is. Yep, mine was a damn fool but I loved him. Seems I remember my mom saying that all men were damn fools and that I'd be better off if I left town and became a nun. But after I met Jacob all that changed. One look into those eyes and I was a goner."

JoAnna grinned. "I know how you feel. My mom didn't like my husband either. But then again, she has a problem with all men, including my father. I think death was a release for him."

Lydia looked at JoAnna and frowned. "Your father is gone?"

"Yes. He died about six months ago. How about your parents?"

Lydia's faced darkened and JoAnna hoped her question wasn't too personal.

"They're both gone. They died in a car wreck several years ago. It's just me now. I don't have any brothers or sisters." Lydia looked wistfully across the room and through the window into the backyard. "They didn't have much but they had a small life insurance policy. I was able to use it to buy this trailer and the lot it sits on. It's a good thing. I don't make much at the diner and with Jacob gone I'd probably be homeless if it wasn't for that insurance money. At least I know I'll always have somewhere to live."

JoAnna felt her heart sink. Paul had been right when he told her she really didn't have any idea how hard some people had it.

"It's a really nice place. Very cozy. And this couch looks comfy," JoAnna said as she walked over and sat down.

Lydia went into the kitchen and looked in the refrigerator. When she realized she didn't have anything to make for dinner, she closed the door and walked over to the counter. She leaned down on her elbows so she could see under the cabinets into the living room.

"You know, I usually just bring something home from the diner to have for dinner. Old Charlie, the owner, is good about letting us have some leftovers from what he makes during the day. Usually just charges us half price, but sometimes he gives it to us for free. There's one other server and a few people that work in the kitchen. Today I didn't bring anything home but I'm sure we can whip something up for dinner tonight."

"If you've got eggs and bacon, we can make breakfast." JoAnna got up and walked to the kitchen. "I'm not much of a cook, but I can make that. Cooking dinner is the least I can do. I really appreciate you letting me stay here tonight. I don't think I could have taken another night of Cooper trying to get into my room."

Lydia frowned. "He's big time creepy. I don't think he has a single friend in town. He's never been married, either. Hell, I've never even seen him with a girl." She walked back to the refrigerator to check for eggs and bacon.

"I can make French toast too, as long as you have one of those little bottles of that vanilla stuff."

"Vanilla?" Lydia walked to another cabinet. After a few seconds of searching she found a small bottle of vanilla extract. "How the hell did you get in there?" she said to the little bottle, surprised that she had found it.

JoAnna made French toast and bacon. She and Lydia sat at the small kitchen table and had dinner as the windows on the back of the trailer to glowed orange from the setting sun. When finished they sat down on the couch and tried to find something on the television. After clicking through a few channels, they gave up and turned down the volume and decided to talk about their husbands instead. After a few minutes, Lydia remembered the bottle of whiskey.

"Say, I forgot that I promised you some whiskey. I've haven't been snockered in a long time." She winked at JoAnna. "I'll be right back."

When Lydia returned, she sat a glass jar with a brass-colored lid down on the table in front of the couch. The jar was full of a clear liquid. JoAnna looked at it as a puzzled expression washed over her face. "Water?" she said halfheartedly as Lydia sat looking at her, already aware that her new houseguest had no idea what was in the jar.

"Oh no, honey. That ain't water." Lydia cocked her head and raised an eyebrow. "You're a city girl, aren't you?"

JoAnna felt her cheeks warm. "Well… yeah. I was born and raised in the city. Spartanburg, South Carolina to be exact." She looked at Lydia and then at the jar full of what she thought was water. Lydia chuckled.

"Well girl, in the city I'm sure whiskey is brown and comes in a bottle with some old man's name on it, but out here in the country whiskey comes in a Mason jar and is as clear as the day is long." Lydia got up and went to the kitchen. She returned with two red plastic cups. "That jar is full of corn liquor and it will knock you on your ass."

JoAnna looked at the jar and then at Lydia while trying to hide her astonishment. "Moonshine? You mean, like, the illegal kind?" She wondered what her mother would think if she knew her daughter was sitting in a mobile home in the middle of swampland getting ready to drink illegal whiskey. She couldn't help but smile at the thought of it.

"Yep. Illegal. No such thing as legal Moonshine. That's what makes it taste so damn good. My husband got a few jars of this from, well, you know, a friend of a friend of a friend. That's how that always goes. He knew the guy, and he knew it was safe. You can't drink this stuff unless you know where it comes from. You can go blind."

"Blind?" JoAnna gave up trying to hide her astonishment. She was in uncharted territory and enjoying every minute of it.

"Yep," replied Lydia. "Jacob always said you had to know if the guy that made it used copper line to distill it. You'll hear wives' tales about Shiners using old car radiators in their stills. The lead gets into the liquor and will cause people to go blind after they drink it."

"Holy shit," replied JoAnna, feeling like an outlaw. Here she was sitting in a trailer about to drink illegal whiskey that if made wrong could cause her to go blind. Just the thought of it lifted her spirits. This was the best she had felt since coming to Solomon.

Lydia looked at her and winked. "But I know this is good stuff. Jacob and I had a few shots last New Year's Eve. I sure made him happy that night if you know what I mean. The damn fool..." Her smile didn't match the sad look in her eyes. JoAnna knew Lydia missed her husband as much as she missed Paul.

Lydia poured a small amount of the whiskey into each of their plastic cups and then sat down beside JoAnna on the couch. JoAnna picked up the cup and took a sniff of the contents. She eyed Lydia and then they tapped their cups together to make a toast.

"To our husbands."

"The damn fools," replied JoAnna before downing the Moonshine in one quick swallow. Lydia followed suit and then waited for JoAnna's response.

"Well?" She watched JoAnna lick her lips. "What do you think?"

"It hardly has any taste at all. It almost tastes like water, but it has some sort of sweet aftertaste that I can't place." JoAnna put her cup back down on the table. "Maybe another shot will help me figure it out."

Lydia smiled and poured each of them another shot. They tapped their cups together again and downed the shots just as fast as they had the first ones. After the second shot JoAnna began to feel the warmth spreading through her body.

Lydia sat her cup down on the table. "We gotta be careful, Jo. This stuff will sneak up on us. That's what happened to me last New Year's Eve. I only had about four or five shots before Jacob said I started acting like a stripper in a titty bar. Like I said, I made him happy that night. But all I remember was the hangover the next morning."

JoAnna felt the heat of the Moonshine creeping through her arms and legs and decided to take Lydia's advice and slow down. She sat her cup down on the table and leaned back on the couch. "Tell me about Jacob. How did you two meet each other?"

Lydia leaned back on the couch still holding her empty plastic cup. She stared up at the ceiling lost in thought.

"Oh... You know... High school. You know us country girls... We don't know how to do much except get married young and have a baby. Jacob and I got married right after high school, then I got pregnant. Usually it's the other way around but we got married first. He said he would love me forever." Lydia rolled her plastic cup around in her hand, then looked over at JoAnna. "Yep, he said he would love me forever. The damn fool... I've got a picture of him right here." Lydia reached over to the small end table beside the couch and then handed JoAnna a framed photo.

She studied the handsome young man in the photo and then looked at Lydia and smiled.

"He's good looking," she said before handing photo back to Lydia. "You got pregnant? What happened? I mean, if that's okay to ask. I don't want to be too nosey." JoAnna looked at her plastic cup, silently wishing it was full of the corn liquor.

"I lost the baby. They didn't know why. Just Mother Nature's way of telling us how stupid we were, I guess. It really bothered Jacob. It bothered me too, but we moved on and got over it." Lydia sat her cup down on the table next to the Mason jar. "It was probably for the best." JoAnna noticed the glossy film building in her eyes. "But the worst part..." Lydia leaned back in her chair and grew silent.

"What was the worst part?"

"Oh, nothing, I guess."

"It's okay. You can tell me."

Lydia looked over at JoAnna as tears puddled in her eyes. "I can't have children anymore. Something happened, and the doctor said I would never be able to have another child."

"Oh Lydia, I'm so sorry. I don't know what to say." Then she thought about her own ordeal, and how it gave her and Lydia one more thing in common.

"I know you're probably not going to believe this, but I lost a baby too. Paul and I, we lost our first child. He was stillborn. I think it was what caused Paul to…"

Lydia looked at JoAnna as her face grew serious. She reached up and wiped the tears from her eyes. "Caused him to what?"

"Well, I didn't tell you before that when I said I lost my husband, I meant I lost him to suicide. He killed himself. Right up in the attic of our house in Charleston. I was the one that found him."

Lydia's mouth dropped open. "Holy fucking shit." She looked down into her lap and then back at JoAnna. "I'm sorry. I didn't mean to say that."

"It's okay. Holy fucking shit just about sums it up."

"Why didn't you tell me before?"

JoAnna reached for her plastic cup. She needed something to hold in her hands. "I don't normally tell people about it. I mean, I guess it's kind of embarrassing. But yes, he killed himself. Just like his father did."

Lydia gasped. "His father committed suicide too?"

"When Paul was twelve," JoAnna replied as she stared blankly across the room.

"I'll be damned…" Lydia placed her plastic cup back on the table.

"That's the word Paul used. He thought his father was damned." JoAnna rubbed the outside of her cup with her thumb. "He told me once that he thought something *got* his father. I didn't really know what he meant, but I think he thought the Devil got him or something like that. The man blew a hole in his chest out in the shed in their backyard. Paul found him lying in a wheelbarrow."

Lydia was speechless. She looked at JoAnna and then at the Mason jar. "I think we've both earned another shot."

"I think you're right," replied JoAnna as she reached forward and slid her cup towards the jar. Lydia poured two shots and after they downed them, she got up and checked the lock on the front door.

"I better make sure the door is locked before we have any more to drink. Pretty soon we're not gonna be able to walk much less work the lock on the door."

Lydia walked into the kitchen, bumping into the edge of the counter as she went. She retrieved a large bag of potato chips from the cupboard and then went back to the living room, weaving slightly as she walked. Once back on the couch, she tore open the bag of chips and held it out to JoAnna, who reached in and grabbed a handful. As JoAnna crunched on the potato chips, she felt her head swirl. But the haze from the alcohol was beginning to ease her nervousness about asking Lydia to tell her about Madam Valentine and Isabelle Pearl. And JoAnna knew that she had to ask. She knew that she had to know the story behind both women.

"Say, about that palm reader lady, Madam Valentine. What's her story?" JoAnna suddenly felt the room tilt and contort. She could feel her heart beating in her chest, pumping the alcohol through her body.

Lydia leaned back on the couch and licked the salt off her fingers. "She's something, ain't she? Most people don't believe in that stuff but I'm telling you she's got a gift. Or a curse depending on the way you look at it."

"She knew about Paul's suicide and his father's. There's no way she could have known that if she wasn't for real. I didn't even tell you until just now." Her eyes tried to focus on Lydia's. "And she knew I had lost a child. I wasn't a believer in that stuff but after seeing her, I think I am. No, I know I am." JoAnna leaned back on the couch and stifled a hiccup.

"What else did she tell you?" Lydia tried to hide the fact that she already knew the answer to her question.

JoAnna paused. She didn't have the courage yet to mention Isabelle Pearl. "Let's have another shot and I'll tell you." She picked up her cup and tapped the bottom of it on the table.

"You city girls sure do like to drink." Lydia said as she poured. "But I'm warning you. We better ease up after this shot or we'll pass out right here on the couch." After they took another shot, JoAnna looked at Lydia. It was getting harder to focus her eyes.

"She said there is a lady in town named Isabelle Pearl that can, you know, help people like me with their grief. But she didn't say how." JoAnna flinched as another hiccup followed her words. She placed her hand over her mouth and apologized.

"Do you miss your husband? Do you miss Paul?" Lydia felt her head swirl as she spoke. She knew she could handle her alcohol better than JoAnna but it was beginning to catch up with her.

"Yes."

"No, I mean do you really, really miss him? As in you can't go on without him. Is he all you ever think about?"

JoAnna turned to Lydia, her face warm and flush. "I miss him so much, Lydia. Sometimes I think if I could just hold him one more time, if I could just feel his touch one more time, I'd be okay. I need to feel his arms around me."

Lydia's eyes met JoAnna's. "You need Isabelle Pearl. She helped me and that's why I know everything is going to be okay."

"What can she do? Is she like Madam Valentine? Is she going to tell my fortune or something? Madam Valentine wouldn't tell me. But she did say that Isabelle Pearl's fee is different for every person. What does that mean?" JoAnna could feel the liquor catching up with her. She hadn't been this drunk since the night she and Paul went out on the town after they moved into their apartment in Charleston.

"It means she doesn't work for money. She gives you something you love but then she demands something you love in return. It's different for every person."

JoAnna didn't reply. After a few seconds, she finally spoke. "I need one more shot."

Lydia poured them each another shot, almost emptying the jar. "This is our last one, girl. After this we'll go to our happy place." JoAnna reached for the cup and downed the shot quickly, smacking her lips at the near tasteless liquid.

"And Madam Valentine said a young girl had just gone to see this Isabelle lady. She didn't say, but it sounded like she was talking about you." JoAnna felt the couch yaw underneath her.

Lydia's eyes glazed over. "I can't tell you. If I do, it might undo what she did for me. Tomorrow I'll drive you to her house. You need her. Trust me on this, and you won't regret it." Lydia extended her index finger from around her cup and pointed at JoAnna, then tipped the cup to her lips again to get the last few drops. She dropped her cup in her lap and passed out cold, followed by JoAnna. For Lydia the night would be long and dreamless. JoAnna Stedford, however, would not be so lucky.

10

JoAnna was lying on the couch alone with her legs curled up close to her body. Lydia, she figured, had gotten up in the middle of the night and gone to her bedroom. The trailer was silent.

She scanned the dark room moving only her eyes. Draped over the back of the couch was an old throw and she quickly reached up and pulled it down over her body leaving only half her face uncovered. Then she grew still again as her eyes continued to scan the room. She could see down the length of the long narrow hallway that led to the bedroom on the other end of the trailer. Moonlight poured in through the windows, painting the edges of the shades silver. All the lights were off, but the moonlight was enough to illuminate the interior of the trailer. The only movement came from the pendulum of an old Coo Coo clock hanging on the wall.

Movement at the end of the hall caught JoAnna's eyes. When she saw the shadowy outline of a person standing in the bedroom door, goosebumps rose on her arms. Then whoever it was began walking slowly down the hallway towards her.

JoAnna's entire body tingled as she watched the dark figure move down the hallway, getting closer to her with every step. When she saw the face, she recognized it as the face of the man she had seen in the framed picture. It was the face of Lydia's dead husband.

JoAnna gasped and sat upright on the coach. She looked around quickly and saw there was no one in the room other than Lydia, who was still passed out on the other end of the couch. She placed her hand on her forehead, closed her eyes and tried to get control of her nerves. Her breathing was fast and she could feel her heart pounding in her temples.

The liquor was burning in her bowels. Trying not to wake Lydia, she got off the couch and made her way to the bathroom. A small night light plugged into the outlet near the sink provided all the light she needed. The bathroom was small but very clean, proving once again that Lydia took pride in her home.

Once finished, she got up and adjusted herself, then stepped in front of the mirror to examine her face in the dim glow of the night light. She had passed out from the Moonshine before removing her makeup and eyeliner and now her eyes were puffy as a result. She shook her head in disgust and then opened the door to the bathroom. Her makeup would have to wait until morning.

Once back in the kitchen, JoAnna retrieved another cup from the cabinet and poured herself some water from the faucet. Her mouth was dry and pasty, and after a few sips she leaned forward and pulled the sheer drapes open enough to see into the front yard. She looked at the old birdbath sitting in the middle of the yard, and then her eyes followed the gravel driveway out to the road.

Lydia's trailer sat back off the road with woods on each side of the lot. No other houses or trailers were visible from her front yard. JoAnna thought to herself that the privacy was probably nice to have until the sun went down. After that, she knew the trailer would seem lonely and isolated. She wondered how a young, attractive girl like Lydia could feel safe living in a trailer all by herself in such a secluded location. Just as she was about to return to the couch, her eyes caught movement at the edge of the tree line near the road.

JoAnna watched as someone moved along the road in front of the trailer. She told herself that even though it was a little odd given the hour, there was nothing particularly wrong with a person walking along the road at night. But then the person stopped and turned to look directly at the trailer, then after a few seconds stepped into the yard and started walking across the yard. JoAnna froze and watched the man move across the moonlit yard. When he got closer, she recognized his face. It was the face of the young man she had just dreamed about. It was the face of Lydia's dead husband Jacob.

JoAnna gasped and let go of the drapes. She turned quickly in the dark kitchen and started towards the couch, only to run into Lydia who had awakened and was on her way to the bathroom.

"Damn girl, where's the fire?" Lydia put both hands across her abdomen. "I can't talk now, I'm about to pee in my pajamas." She left JoAnna in the kitchen and moved quickly to the bathroom. Once she returned JoAnna grabbed her by the arm.

"There's a man standing in the yard," JoAnna whispered as if she didn't want the man outside to hear her. "I was getting a drink of water and I saw him walk from the road into your yard."

Lydia rubbed the sleep out of her eyes. "Are you sleepwalking, Jo? Moonshine has been known to make a person do that."

"No! I'm not sleepwalking. I got up to go to the bathroom and then went to get a drink of water. That's when I saw him through the window." She wanted to tell Lydia who the man looked like but thought better of it. Her mind could be playing tricks on her. The dream had been one thing, but she knew that the man in the yard was not a dream and that there was no way it could be Jacob.

Lydia eyed JoAnna again and then walked over to the kitchen window. She pulled the drape to the side and looked out into the yard, scanning from the deck all the way out to the road. The only thing she saw in the yard was the old birdbath.

"Looks like we're all alone. I don't see anything in the yard except my old birdbath. Do you want me to go get my shotgun and go out there and shoot it for you?"

"I know I saw a man," snapped JoAnna. "He was right there close to the kitchen window. He walked into your yard from the road."

"Well, he's gone now so I'm going back to bed. My head is already killing me. You can stretch out on the couch. I'll get you a blanket." Lydia walked off towards the bedroom. She returned with a large quilt and tossed it on the couch. She looked at JoAnna standing in the kitchen, still terrified and shaking in the darkness.

"Hey girl." Lydia walked over to JoAnna. "You look like you've seen a ghost. Just crawl under that quilt and you'll be fine. We can sleep for a few more hours and then have Tylenol for breakfast. And by the way, I wasn't kidding when I said I had a shotgun. My daddy raised me to know how to take care of myself. If anyone is out there and tries to get in, I'll blow their fucking head off. Don't worry about it, okay?"

JoAnna looked at Lydia and then back at the kitchen window. "Okay. But I know I saw him."

"You probably did see somebody. I get crazies walking down my road all the time. About a mile down the way is Willie Cobb's trailer. I think he sells things. You know, drugs and stupid shit like that.

People go and come at all hours, but they never bother me. You might have seen someone going down there to see him. And I guess they could have wandered into the yard."

JoAnna looked at the kitchen window one more time, then put her hand on her forehead. She closed her eyes and exhaled. "Maybe you're right."

In the morning the weather had turned cloudy and the window shades were awash with hazy gray sunlight. JoAnna sat up on the couch and felt her heart beating in her temples. It was the worst headache she had ever had. She got up and used the bathroom and then went to the kitchen to see if she could make coffee and find something to ease the pounding in her head. She was searching one of the cabinets when Lydia walked into the kitchen.

"Damn homemade whiskey. It'll do it every time. I feel like someone is trying to jackhammer their way out of my head."

"Tell me about it. The coffee will help though. Where's the headache medicine?"

Lydia opened a cabinet next to the refrigerator and handed JoAnna a bottle of Tylenol. "We ate all my breakfast stuff last night. There's a fast-food joint up the road from the diner, on the edge of town. I could go get us some biscuits or something. They've got a drive-thru. I'll go take a shower and throw on some makeup. You can take a shower and freshen up while I go get the biscuits."

"That sounds great," JoAnna said. "And it's my treat."

Lydia poured herself a cup of coffee and closed her eyes after she took a sip. "Whew... I haven't had a headache like this in a long time, Jo."

"Worse than the day after New Year's Eve?" JoAnna said as she raised her cup to her lips.

Lydia smiled and seemed to drift away. "I'd say just as bad. But he sure was happy that night. That boy sure loved to separate me from my panties."

"Sounds like Paul," JoAnna quipped. "I think all husbands are horndogs, but I can't imagine life without them."

"Me neither, and I refuse to." They both looked at each other and JoAnna could see the resolve in Lydia's eyes.

"I'll get a shower," Lydia finally said, breaking the silence. She took her coffee cup and went back to the bedroom.

JoAnna finished her cup of coffee and poured herself another one, then rummaged through her purse until she found some money for the biscuits. She knew she had two phone calls to make and figured she would wait until Lydia went for the biscuits to call her mother. But first she needed to get an update on her car.

Jared answered on the second ring. "I'll have your tires by the end of the day, Miss. Stedford. Pike should have the alignment finished in the morning. We ought to have you on the road by noon tomorrow."

"That's quicker than I had hoped." JoAnna smiled and shifted the phone to her other ear. "I really appreciate it. I'll call you in the morning to check on it."

Lydia walked into the kitchen and placed her cup in the sink. "Good news?"

"Yep. They should have my car ready by lunch time tomorrow," she said, suddenly feeling embarrassed. "I mean my mother's car. I could never afford a car like that. And the same goes for her. She only has it because my father died and left her some insurance money."

"No need to be ashamed. Like I said before that's how I got this trailer. I'd be homeless without my parents' insurance money."

"I guess parents are smarter than we think."

"Yep. It's one of those dirty little secrets." Lydia grabbed her car keys and JoAnna handed her a twenty-dollar bill. "Just get me whatever you're getting. After I take a shower and I'll call my mom." JoAnna rolled her eyes. "Not looking forward to it. I'll be lucky if she isn't on her way out here ten minutes after we hang up. I completely forgot to call her last night."

"Tell her that's my fault." Lydia walked towards the door. "Tell her some country girl you met in a roadside diner got you drunk on homemade liquor. She'll understand."

"Oh yeah, she'll understand." A crooked grinned crossed her face. "I'd love to get her a few jars of that stuff so she could pass them out at her next Sunday brunch. I'd pay good money to watch her friends get drunk on it."

Lydia laughed. "Corn liquor can loosen the lips, that's for sure." She grabbed her purse. "Lock the door behind me, Jo." Once Lydia was gone, JoAnna took a shower, got dressed and called her mother.

"Start talking, young lady." Maxine huffed into the phone. "Why haven't you called me?"

"I'm sorry Mom. Everything is okay. I just forgot to call you last night. I met a girl at the diner. She lives alone, and she invited me to stay the night with her. She's really nice, about my age, and believe it or not she lost her husband too. He died in a motorcycle wreck. The motel I was staying in was kind of creepy and it was the only one in town so I accepted her offer and slept on her couch last night. Don't be mad." JoAnna winced as the words came out of her mouth.

"And my car?" replied Maxine, apparently accepting JoAnna's story.

"The guy at the garage said I should be on my way by noon tomorrow." JoAnna waited through the long silence that followed. Finally, her mother spoke.

"Tomorrow at noon," Maxine said, her voice laced with disbelief. "And who is this girl you're are staying with? A complete stranger? Are you crazy?" JoAnna couldn't see the frown that shot across her mother's face. "I'm sorry, sweetie. I didn't mean that. It's just... It's just that a mother doesn't like to hear that her only daughter is staying with a stranger in some lost town in the middle of nowhere."

"Mom, it's okay. Her name is Lydia. You'd like her." JoAnna knew that was unlikely. Unless Lydia had married for money and knew how to play Canasta, JoAnna knew her mother would have little use for her.

"She's really nice, Mom. She invited me over to her place when I told her about my motel. We cooked some dinner last night and just sat around and talked. It was nice to talk to someone my own age, and very comforting to talk to someone that has lost a husband."

"Suicide?"

"No. I told you. A motorcycle accident."

"That's sounds terrible," Maxine said before shifting the conversation. "You'll be on the road tomorrow? I'm telling you JoAnna, if you're not on the road tomorrow I'm coming out there to get you. Do you understand?"

"Yes, Mother." JoAnna looked up at the ceiling and tried to stay calm.

"I love you sweetie. Call me tomorrow and give me an update. And tell, what was her name? Lydia? Tell Lydia thank you from me."

"I will, Mom. I'll call you tomorrow when the car is ready so you can talk to them about the bill."

Lydia returned about ten minutes after JoAnna got off the phone with her mother. She had a bag full of biscuits, enough for them to have two biscuits apiece. They each poured another cup of coffee and sat down at the small kitchen table to eat.

"So… This Isabelle Pearl lady," JoAnna said reluctantly after she finished her first biscuit. "Do you think I should go see her?" Lydia finished chewing her bite of biscuit before she replied.

"You said you can't live without him. You said that all you need is to feel his arms around you. If you're that consumed with grief then you need Isabelle Pearl. She, well… She can help you deal with it." Lydia took a drink of her coffee and another bite of her biscuit. JoAnna watched her eat, certain Lydia had more to say.

"Deal with it?"

"She helped me, and I know that pretty soon everything is going to be alright."

JoAnna pulled the bag of biscuits to her and reached in for another one. She removed a small Styrofoam container that contained a biscuit covered with gravy. She flipped the box open and grinned at the contents. "Mmmm…" She cut off a piece of biscuit and sopped it in the gravy in the bottom of the container.

"What does pretty soon mean?"

"It means that everything is going to be okay. It just takes a little time." Lydia pulled another biscuit from the bag. This one was a country-fried steak. JoAnna hesitated and then took a sip of coffee. She wasn't sure how Lydia would take what she was about to say.

"Last night, you know when I saw that guy in the yard? Well, I know I was probably half asleep and had just had a wicked nightmare, but the guy looked familiar. I mean, it was dark, but the moon was out and it was bright enough to see his face. He walked right up to the trailer, and that was when I knew I'd seen him somewhere before. Somewhere in, somewhere in town I guess." JoAnna let this hang in the air while she took a bite of her gravy biscuit.

Lydia turned her head towards JoAnna as her chewing slowed and then stopped.

"You'd seen him before? Where?" Then her face flashed with anger. "It wasn't that creep Cooper was it? He knows where I live but he doesn't know you're staying with me. What a fucking creep! I'll bet he was walking down to Willie's trailer to buy meth. He's a damn…"

"It wasn't Cooper."

Lydia started chewing again and looked at JoAnna with

apprehension. "Well, who else in town would you recognize? I mean, you know old Ray. And Jared… You probably saw Pike at the garage. And you know Cooper. Do you know anyone else in town?" Lydia was afraid of what she was going to say next.

"Well, I met a Sheriff's deputy at the Swamp Fox Inn, but it wasn't him in the yard last night."

"Then who was it?"

"I dunno. He just looked familiar." JoAnna glanced quickly at the picture frame sitting on the table by the couch but forced her eyes away from it when she saw Lydia's reaction.

Lydia looked over at the picture and then quickly back at JoAnna. "That's not funny. That's not one damn bit funny. Why would you imply something like that? I've been nice to you." Lydia then got up from the table and walked over to the window by the front door. She peered through the drapes at the front yard now bathed in the soft gray light of the overcast morning. "You're shitting me. Right? Is this a joke? Are you fucking with me, Jo?"

JoAnna felt a blade of panic cut through her stomach. She got up and walked over to Lydia. "I would never joke about something like that. I'm just saying it looked like him. But I was still drunk so I don't know what I saw. By the time you came into the kitchen he was gone. For all I know, I could have dreamed the whole thing. I'm so sorry. I've got to learn how to keep my big mouth shut. Paul always said I talk too much."

Lydia looked through the drapes again and then at JoAnna, who was on the verge of crying. But when their eyes met, the look Lydia was giving her struck JoAnna as strange. It wasn't anger. If JoAnna didn't know better, she would have sworn that the look in Lydia's eyes looked more like hope than anger.

"It looked like him? Be straight with me, Jo."

"I am being straight with you. But like I said, my head was still spinning from the whiskey."

"She said everything was going to be okay," Lydia whispered as she turned and peered through the window.

11

Lydia walked down the hall towards the kitchen dressed in her server uniform. JoAnna had cleaned off the table and was washing a few dishes in the sink.

"I've got to work from noon until midnight tonight. It's like that every Wednesday. The finishing mill gets a lot of trucks, starting in the afternoon and going until around midnight. Charlie likes to get all the business he can since those truckers are usually hungry. It's the only night we're open late. I know you'll be bored all day but you can stay here again tonight if they don't finish with your car. I had fun last night. It's been a long time since I had some nice girl talk."

JoAnna smiled. "I had fun last night too, and thanks for the invite for tonight. I guess I'll ride to the diner with you and then maybe walk down to the garage and see how it's going with the car. Then I can come back to the diner and have some lunch. I thought that…" JoAnna paused and looked at Lydia. "I thought that maybe I'd go see this Isabelle Pearl lady. It sounds stupid, but for some reason I keep thinking that I should go."

"It's not stupid," Lydia replied. "But if you want to go see her, I'd wait until later in the afternoon. She'll serve you dinner and you'll have to spend the night. Her house is a little on the spooky side if you know what I mean. It sits across from an old house that used to be a funeral home. That was back when Solomon was a lot bigger than it is now."

"Spend the night?" JoAnna said as her eyes grew wide. "Why would I need to spend the night?"

"If you want her to help you, you'll have to spend the night. That's just how it goes."

JoAnna frowned. "I… I don't know. Maybe I should just stay here all day and tonight. I mean, if you don't mind."

"You know I don't mind, Jo. But you and I need to have a talk now that we're both sober. I've got an hour before I have to be at work." Lydia motioned at the small kitchen table. When they sat down, she looked directly into JoAnna's eyes with a seriousness that JoAnna found alarming.

"Listen, girl. I like you. I wouldn't invite you to spend the night and then share my husband's last jar of corn liquor with you if I didn't like you. You and I have a lot in common so here's the story. I'm going to tell you about this and then if you still want to go see Isabelle, I'll drive you out there myself. But I'm warning you, there is no turning back once you're inside her house."

JoAnna swallowed hard. "Okay. Tell me."

Lydia took a deep breath. "There are some people in town that say Isabelle Pearl is a witch. Some old timers around this town even say she's the Devil, all dressed up in a pretty package. Or maybe she's the Devil's wife, but whatever she is I swear she's about the most beautiful woman you'll ever see. There are people in town that have gone to see her, and there are people around here that want to burn her house to the ground with her inside it. I'm part of the first group. I went to see her and I know everything is going to be all right for me."

JoAnna leaned back in her chair as sarcasm blanketed her face. "Come on… A witch? The Devil? You're full of it. I'm from out of town and you're just trying to mess with me. Or are you just trying to get me back for when I told you I thought the guy in the yard last night looked like your husband."

"I'm not messing with you, Jo. I really shouldn't be telling you any of this. But I like you. Like I said, you and I have a lot in common."

"The Devil…" JoAnna tried to suppress her laughter. "My daddy always said if the Devil ever showed up on the earth that he'd be dressed up like a politician. He never said anything about the Devil being a beautiful woman living in an old house in a little town like Solomon." JoAnna waited for Lydia to laugh at her joke but the smile faded from her face when she realized she was serious.

"There's more if you want to hear it. Speak now if you don't."

JoAnna dropped her hands into her lap. "Tell me."

"That old building across from her house, the one that used to be a funeral home, I think it has something to do with when this all started. It all happened a long time ago, back when the finishing mill was three times the size it is now and a lot more people lived here. There was a huge fire in one of the buildings out at the mill that killed over a hundred people. Some of them were burned alive, and the rest died from the smoke or when the building collapsed on them. That old funeral home was the only one in town and it had a hard time handling all the bodies. People were coming and going all day and half the night for over a week trying to pay their respects. The story goes that they had coffins set up in all the rooms of the funeral home, even in the basement. My grandfather told me all this years ago. He worked at the mill at the time and some of his friends were killed in the fire."

JoAnna brought her hand to her mouth. "That's terrible!"

"It's more terrible than you can imagine, Jo. Most folks believe that all that grief drew something evil to the town." Lydia paused. "Do you want to hear more? I'm warning you. By the time you hear the rest of the story you'll be so fucking scared you won't leave this trailer."

JoAnna crossed her arms in front of her stomach and leaned forward towards the table. "Keep going," she whispered.

"They say that some of the people that died in that fire showed up in town months later, long after they had been buried. That's what my grandfather told me before he died and he wouldn't have lied to me. He said it scared the townspeople so fucking bad that some of them just up and moved away. And then word got out that some wives of the dead mill workers had visited Isabelle. That's when people started to figure out what she was, and what she could do for them."

"What she could do for them?" JoAnna said.

"You gotta understand the grief, Jo. They say it consumed the entire town. Almost everybody in town lost someone in that fire. Some lost friends, others lost family members. My grandfather said it was just terrible. He said the townsfolk believed that the grief in Solomon was so great that it woke the dead. After that, the town just started to decline. The mill didn't rebuild, and they took a hit to their business. But Isabelle stayed. She stayed in her old house and she's still out there today."

"Wait a minute," JoAnna said. "What do you mean she's still there today? You said that was a long time ago."

"Yep. It was. And she's still just as young and beautiful as she was when they laid all those bodies out in that funeral home."

JoAnna shook her head and scoffed. "Please tell me this is all some sort of joke. You can't be serious. You're telling me that this Isabelle Pearl lady is some sort of witch, or the Devil, or some kind of hobgoblin that never ages and can raise the dead? And I thought I was the one that was crazy. Maybe I'm not the one that needs therapy around here. Maybe you do, Lydia."

Lydia looked at JoAnna. She knew that what she was about to say would convince JoAnna that she was telling the truth.

"It was him, Jo. The guy you saw last night in my yard was my husband. Isabelle said he would come. I just didn't know when. She said that sometimes it takes a little time."

A shiver rushed down JoAnna's back. "Lydia, you have got to be crazy. Please tell me this is a joke. I'm a good sport. Fair is fair. Please tell me this is all just a load of bullshit. Now is the time to yell gotcha and tell me this is a joke."

Lydia shook her head. "Ray's been dead for three years, Jo. The old guy that helped you when you wrecked your car, the one that took you to Jared's garage and the Swamp Fox Inn... He's been dead for over three years. He lived out on the main road just outside of town and ran his gas station with his wife. When he died, his wife was so grief stricken and heartbroken that she went to see Isabelle."

JoAnna rolled her eyes. "You're certifiable, Lydia. You need a room at Morgan."

"I'm not crazy, Jo. Everybody knows what Isabelle does. They call her Wicked Izzy, and they know exactly what she does. And they know about Ray. They either deal with it or leave town. And there are others in town like Ray. I can't tell you who, but you'll know. You'll figure it out. The people that are left in town now have just learned to live with it. Some choose to use her services, others don't. Like I said, I'm one of the ones that went to see her, and from what you saw last night it seems to be working. Soon I'll be with my husband again, thanks to her."

JoAnna felt bile crawling up her throat. She was sitting in a trailer with a crazy woman so sick with grief from losing her husband that she believed he had returned from the grave. It was time for her to get out of the trailer, get to her car, and get out of Solomon as soon as possible.

"I just talked to Ray yesterday but you're telling me he's been dead for three years?" JoAnna looked into Lydia's eyes and tried to hide her anger. "I've heard enough, Lydia. Can you please take me to the garage? I need to check on my car. They may finish it early, and if they do, I'll be able to leave. I really appreciate you letting me stay here last night."

Lydia frowned and looked down at the table. JoAnna was about to get up and get her purse when Lydia reached out and touched her hand.

"Jo, really, it's okay. I know you think I'm crazy. Hell, I'd be running for the hills if I came to this little town and someone told me a story like that. But just trust me, she'll help you. And I'll understand if you really don't want to go see her. Maybe you should just try to move on, to learn to live without him. I thought about trying that, and I made a go of it but after a month I just couldn't take it. I'm all alone in this shitty little town, my parents are gone, and all I have is this trailer. Jacob was the only person I had in the world. In the end I knew I had no choice but to go see Wicked Izzy."

JoAnna's heart skipped in her chest. *Wicked Izzy...* The words seemed to float in the air between them. She looked at Lydia's hand on top of hers and tried to calm herself. After a few seconds she asked the only question that she could think of.

"Madam Valentine said Isabelle Pearl doesn't work for money and that her price is different for everyone. What was your price? What did you have to give her?" JoAnna knew she would have her car soon and could then get out of Solomon forever. Maybe the best way to handle Lydia was to just go along with the story for now.

Lydia pulled her hand away from JoAnna's and leaned back in her chair.

"I don't know. That's the bad part, Jo. I don't know what her price is, but I'll find out soon enough. I don't know what she will want from you, and neither will you until it's time to pay. But I do know that it's different for everyone. And sometimes a person pays soon, and sometimes years pass before Izzy settles up with them." Lydia smiled weakly and looked down into her lap at her folded hands. "I just figured that whatever it is it will be worth it. He was all I had. What else do I have to lose? What else can she take?"

Outside the rain poured down. JoAnna could hear the raindrops pinging on the sheet metal sides of the trailer and the deep rumble of thunder in the distance. She felt compassion for her friend swell up inside her, then she felt a tiny flicker of hope. What if Lydia was telling the truth?

JoAnna's face softened as she looked at Lydia. "Sometimes that's how I feel. I mean, I do have my mother so I'm not alone like you are, but sometimes she and I don't get along. Until just a week ago we didn't get along at all but things are better between us now. She paid for my year of therapy after Paul's suicide and the stillbirth and then let me borrow her car to come on this trip. Now look at me, sitting here talking about going to see some sort of witch, or whatever, so that I can see my dead husband again. Maybe I'm as crazy as they said I was."

"You're not crazy, Jo. This world is full of strange things. Who knows what's out there? Who knows how Wicked Izzy does it? Who knows where she comes from? I don't. I would go see her if I were you, but it has to be your choice. I know where she lives so if you want to go, I'll take you."

"I think you're as crazy as I am. Maybe we're both sick in the head. You can't possibly tell me this story is true, Lydia. I mean, come on. You really think Jacob is coming back?"

Lydia folded her arms. "I don't think it, I know it."

JoAnna exhaled and looked out the window at the sheets of rain marching across the front yard. "I just… I dunno. Maybe I should just get my car and be on my way."

"Listen, Jo, why don't we take off and I'll drop you at the garage so you can check on your car, then I'll go to work. You can walk over to the diner after you leave the garage. I get a break late in the afternoon to eat supper and I can take you to Isabelle's house on my break. I'll pick you up in the morning. Like I said, you'll have to stay the night with her."

Despite the previous glimmer of hope, JoAnna knew Lydia had to be crazy, and she was amazed at how well she seemed to believe her own story. But she knew there had been a time when she could tell stories almost as wild as Lydia's. She thought about the ghost of Paul's father and how it had been following her around, haunting her dreams, and had even forced her to swerve off the road and almost drive into the swamp canal. Was Lydia crazy? Was she just repeating some old folk tale told to every person that passed through town?

But the same thought still nagged at her. What if Lydia wasn't lying?

Lydia looked at her watch. "We gotta go. I'll drop you at Jared's and then you can come over to the diner, okay? Don't be so terrified, girl," she said as she looked at JoAnna. "It'll be all right. Just forget all about it if you want to."

They got up from the table and grabbed their purses. JoAnna decided to leave her duffel bag just in case Jared wasn't finished with her car and she had to come back to the trailer for the night. It was either that or Cooper at the Swamp Fox Inn. Or if she decided to believe Lydia's story about Isabelle Pearl, she figured her bag would be the last thing she would be concerned with.

Lydia locked the trailer door behind them and they drove to Jared's through the pouring rain. They hardly spoke along the way and in the back of JoAnna's mind the doubts she had about Lydia's story were beginning to wane.

Just one more touch... Did Wicked Izzy have the power to give her that? JoAnna shook her head and felt disgusted with herself. To believe such an outlandish thing surely meant she needed to go back to the Morgan Institute for another year of therapy.

Lydia pulled into the parking lot of the garage and brought her car to a stop. The rain had eased to a light drizzle. She reached up and turned off her windshield wipers and looked at JoAnna sitting sheepishly in the passenger's seat.

"Wicked Izzy lives a few miles down that road," Lydia said as she nodded towards the road that led away from the garage. "You'll see an old barn and a windmill on the left. There's a road right next to the barn. Her house is down that road. It's the only house out there with anyone living in it. If you decide to go, I'll take you."

JoAnna smiled. *She's crazy. But...* She forced the thought from her mind. Lydia's story couldn't be true, but JoAnna knew that ghosts were real. She had proof of that. But Lydia wasn't talking about ghosts.

"Okay. I'll see you at the diner in a little while. I need to call my mother again and give her an update on the car. I mean, it is hers after all. Then I'll come over to the diner."

"Sounds like a deal," replied Lydia.

12

Jared walked in from the service bay wiping his hands with a rag. "Well howdy, Miss Stedford. Your tires should be in this morning. Once we get them, Pike will put them on and align your front end. He's a good kid, but he's never worked on a Mercedes so I told him to be careful with it. That car is worth more than my entire shop."

Just then Pike came in from the service bay and walked across the office to the soda machine. He smiled weakly but tried to hide his face as he walked by JoAnna. He bought a soda and a pack of crackers from the second machine and as he walked back across the office, JoAnna caught sight of his eyes. They were dark and brooding, just like she remembered Ray's eyes had been on the morning she had breakfast with him.

There are others... Lydia's words echoed through her mind as she watched Pike disappear into repair bay.

"That's the best news I've heard since I got here," she said as she smiled at Jared. "I guess I'll come back this afternoon and check on it."

"We'll be here until five," Jared said as an impact wrench rattle loudly in the repair bay.

"Okay. I'll make sure I check in before then."

Sunlight reflected off the glossy film of water on the road as JoAnna walked into the parking lot. She squinted and looked down the road and then back in the direction of the diner. Across the street she noticed an old house with a sign over the front door that read: *Public Library*. She wasn't quite ready to see Lydia again, so she decided to kill some time and check it out. If anything, she could sit down in peace and quiet and at least read a newspaper or maybe a magazine.

The old wood planks in the porch creaked as she climbed the steps and walked up to the door. Once inside an elderly woman with grayish-blue hair and a pair of reading glasses perched on the end of her nose greeted her from a small room off to the right of the entrance.

"Welcome," the woman said as JoAnna stepped into the library. "My name is Sadie. Just help yourself and let me know if I can help you find anything."

"I'm JoAnna. They're working on my car across the street and I just thought I'd come in and look around. You know, just for something to do. I love books."

Sadie beamed. "I do too, dear. Don't let our size fool you. We have lots to choose from. Just have a look around. I'll be right here if you have any questions."

The library was an old house converted for public use. A hallway led away from the front door to the back of the house. JoAnna walked past a roped-off stairway leading upstairs and then followed the hallway to the end where she found a kitchen. A soda machine sat where the refrigerator had once been and a large oblong table covered with an assortment of magazines and a few daily newspapers occupied the middle of the room.

JoAnna walked back down the hallway looking into each room as she went. The combined scent of the hardwood floors and the books reminded her of her love of reading and how much she had always enjoyed going to the library. She stepped into a room and ran her fingers along one of the shelves until she spotted a copy of *The Count of Monte Cristo*. She pulled it from the shelf and sat down in one of the musty easy chairs. After a few minutes of flipping through the pages, she put the book back on the shelf and walked out to Sadie's desk.

"Do you by chance have any books about the history of Solomon?" she asked as Sadie looked up from her desk.

"Well of course we do. First door on the left, then look on the shelves in the far corner. You'll find everything from the history of the town during the Civil War all the way up to books about more recent happenings in town, including public records. You know, land surveying, birth announcements, obituaries and those sorts of things."

"Thank you." JoAnna smiled and turned back towards the

hallway. Then she noticed a short row of framed photos hanging on the wall behind Sadie's desk.

"Those are my esteemed predecessors," Sadie said, glowing with pride. "They took care of the library over the years. They're all gone now and I may be the last in line if business doesn't start picking up soon." Sadie's face took on a wistful look as her eyes traveled across the old photos and then to the hallway that led to the reading rooms.

JoAnna studied the photos for a few seconds and then turned and walked back to the hallway. The books about Solomon where right where Sadie had said they would be. When she found a book entitled *Solomon, NC in the Twentieth Century*, she pulled the book from the shelf and sat down on a small loveseat in front of the window.

Newspaper articles that chronicled the events in Solomon during most of the twentieth century filled the book. Lydia had been right. By the looks of the articles, Solomon had once been a much larger town centered around textile manufacturing but had declined over the decades to become a shadow of its former self.

When she flipped to the chapter about the 1960s, she found what she was looking for. The chapter covered the fire at the finishing mill and was complete with a large black-and-white photo of a building at the mill engulfed in flames. *Over one hundred workers die in the largest industrial fire in the history of North Carolina,* read the caption of the photo. The article carried a date of June 19, 1966.

JoAnna read the story and learned that investigators had traced the fire to the old elevator in the building that housed the bulk chemicals used to color the fabric. The flames had spread so quickly that very few of the third shift workers had been able to escape. JoAnna scanned the list of victims and tried to imagine the grief of the families that had to deal with losing loved ones.

She flipped to the next page of the book and saw an article covering the aftermath of the fire. A photo of the funeral home was at the bottom of the page along with another photo of the street outside the funeral home lined with cars. In the photo JoAnna could see another house across the street from the funeral home. *That must be her house,* she thought as her finger touched the photo. A woman with long blonde hair stood on the porch of the house. Suddenly JoAnna felt like she was being watched and when she looked up from the book Sadie was standing in the doorway, her face clouded with apprehension.

"Is everything okay, dear?"

"Oh, yes," replied JoAnna. "I was just reading about the fire at the finishing mill. So sad... It must have been just terrible for this town."

Sadie's expression darkened. She crossed her arms in front of her chest and took in a deep breath. "I lost my husband in that fire. I remember it like it was yesterday. It's been so many years now. So many years without him... It was such a terrible night. You could walk out in the middle of any street in town and you'd hear the wails of sorrow coming from the open windows of almost every home. Just about everyone in town lost a relative, a spouse or a neighbor."

Sadie reached up and wiped the corner of her eye with her finger. "Look at me. All these years and here I am still tearing up about it." She looked at JoAnna and smiled weakly. "The town never really recovered, you know. It was never the same around here. I was just a young woman, but I knew the town would never get over it. The grief was so heavy it seemed to cover everything like a blanket. We just never got over it."

"I'm so sorry, Miss Sadie. I lost my husband too, a little over a year ago and I'm in town to see if I can find any of his relatives. His parents were born here but he never talked about the rest of his family. I thought it would be nice to reconnect if I could just find them. But so far, no one in town has heard of anyone named Stedford."

Sadie folded her arms and thought about this. Finally, she shook her head and said, "Stedford? I'm sorry, dear. I've never heard of anyone with that name living in this town." But when Sadie said this, JoAnna couldn't help but notice the lack of conviction in her voice. Was the old woman lying to her?

Sadie's voice softened. "I'm so sorry to hear that you lost your husband, dear. It's so hard to be without them, isn't it?" Her eyes left JoAnna as she drifted away, lost in thought about her husband. Then she gathered herself together. "Would you like something to drink? A soda maybe?"

"That would be nice," replied JoAnna. "Let me see if I have some change for the machine."

"Oh, don't worry about that. I don't have to pay that old machine. I'll be right back." Sadie disappeared for a moment and then returned with a can of Coke. She handed it to JoAnna and returned to her place by the door.

"To be honest, you're the first person to come in all week. I don't know how much longer they'll keep this old library open to tell you the truth. It's such a shame. Most people don't have time to sit around a library reading books anymore."

"Well, I love books," replied JoAnna. "And this one is really interesting. I read the article about the fire and then another article about the funeral home and how it was overwhelmed with all of the funerals in the days after the fire."

"Yes, it was. My husband's was one of them." JoAnna watched as sadness clouded Sadie's face again.

"And I saw the photo of the house across from the funeral home. There was a lady on the porch. Let me see if I can find her." JoAnna flipped back several pages until she was looking at the photo again. When she looked up from the book, Sadie was standing in the middle of the room staring at her with a strange look on her face. After a few seconds she walked over and sat down on the edge of the loveseat. She placed her hand on JoAnna's knee and spoke in a soft, hushed tone.

"Are you a believer, dear?"

JoAnna was taken aback by the question and didn't answer immediately. "Yes," she finally replied. "We always went to church when I was growing up. I'm a believer."

Sadie had lived in Solomon all her life and knew what went on in town. She knew what JoAnna might be planning on doing, given that she had lost her husband.

"Everything happens for a reason in this world, JoAnna. Sometimes fate should never be challenged. There are people in this town that don't believe that. Don't you listen to them. She still lives out there in that house even though the funeral home closed years ago. Stay away from her. Don't let anyone in town tell you different. She still looks like she did in that photo and it's been over fifty years. She's evil. Some say she's the wife of the Devil himself. No one goes out there anymore unless they…" Sadie stopped and looked down at the book in JoAnna's lap. When she looked up, JoAnna could see fear flare in the old woman's eyes.

"Just take my advice and stay away from her. If you visit her, it will not go well for you."

JoAnna didn't know how to process what Sadie had just told her. She looked down at the book in her lap and at the photo of Isabelle

Pearl standing on the porch of the house.

"I was told by a girl at the diner that they call her Wicked Izzy, but I believe she said her name is Isabelle Pearl." JoAnna was hoping she could get more out of Sadie about Isabelle as well as the town of Solomon.

"That's what she likes to be called. I've never made her acquaintance and no one really knows what her real name is. I'm an old woman, JoAnna, and I've lived in this town my whole life. Isabelle Pearl was out there in that house when I was a little girl. She was there when I buried my husband, and she's still out there today." Sadie got to her feet and collected herself, then looked down at JoAnna.

"Listen to an old woman, JoAnna. My heart was once as heavy with grief as yours is now. Time will soften it. You'll always miss him, just as I will always miss my husband, but Isabelle Pearl is not the answer. You don't want what she offers."

JoAnna closed the book and rested her hands on the cover. "I don't have any plans to go see her. I spent last night with a girl that works at the diner because that old motel was so scary. She told me about Isabelle Pearl but I didn't believe her. Now I guess I know she was telling me the truth."

"Lydia?" JoAnna saw the frown cross Sadie's face.

"Yes. Her name is Lydia. It was so nice of her to invite me to stay with her. She's all by herself out there in that trailer. I don't think I could have taken another night at the Swamp Fox Inn. Cooper scared the bejesus out me the first night I stayed there. I told Lydia I'd rather go sleep under a bridge than spend another night in that wretched motel so she invited me to stay with her until my car is fixed." JoAnna was hoping that the mention of Lydia living alone in her trailer would spark Sadie into telling her more about her, or maybe her dead husband. But Sadie didn't say anything else about her.

"Cooper? He was the one that scared you at the motel? I've known him since he was a little boy. He was a sweet boy when he was little, but then he grew up and the bottle got hold of him. They know him well down at the Sheriff's office too. I'd say spending the night with a stranger is dangerous, but a night in the Swamp Fox Inn with Cooper in the office is probably worse. You'll stay with Lydia again tonight if your car isn't ready?"

JoAnna couldn't help but wonder if Sadie was asking her this to reaffirm that she wasn't planning on visiting Isabelle Pearl.

"Yes, I left my stuff at her trailer. If my car isn't ready, then I'll be staying with her again tonight. And then I'll leave in the morning. But they said they might have my car ready by this afternoon so hopefully I can leave then."

A look of relief washed over Sadie's face. "That Lydia is a very sweet girl. There's lots of goodness in her heart."

"I like her, and we're close to the same age so that makes it even better." JoAnna looked back down at the book in her lap. Sadie sensed that she wanted to continue reading, so she took this as a cue to return to the front desk.

"Well, I need to get back up front, you know, in case there's a mad rush of people who suddenly want to read *Paradise Lost*." Sadie giggled at her joke. "I'll be at my desk if you need anything."

"Will do," JoAnna said as she flipped a page in the book. She scanned the pages covering the 1970s and saw that Solomon continued to decline during the decade due to the poor economy. Nothing newsworthy happened in the town and the article just carried stories about local farmers or store closings. There was a small article about a palm reader giving a reading to the mayor and JoAnna knew this had to be Madam Valentine, or more likely her grandmother.

JoAnna kept flipping pages. When she came to the section about the 1980s, she traced her finger down the page and found and article dated 1986.

Local man dies in an elevator accident at East Pamlico Printing and Finishing

A local Solomon man, Eli Stedford, died Tuesday, September 9 when he tried to climb out of a stalled freight elevator in annex B of the finishing mill. Investigators say the elevator had stopped between the floors due to a technical malfunction and they believe Mr. Stedford climbed through the escape hatch in the roof of the elevator car in an attempt to free himself. Investigators on the scene believe that Mr. Stedford was standing on the top of the elevator trying to open the hoistway doors when the elevator began to move again. They believe the sudden movement of the elevator car caused Mr. Stedford to lose his balance and fall through the opening between the elevator car and the hoistway wall. First shift workers found his body in the bottom of the hoistway after his wife reported him missing the following day. Mr. Stedford is survived by his wife of four years, Mrs. Nancy Stedford.

JoAnna gasped and threw her hand over her mouth. She skimmed the article again to make sure she had not misunderstood it. Once finished she slammed the book shut and looked around the room, then tossed it to the side and got up from the loveseat. Once in the hall she looked towards the front of the house and then down the hall to the kitchen. She wanted to run out of the library and into the street but didn't want to have to run past Sadie at the front desk.

She walked swiftly down the hall towards the kitchen until she came to the restroom. Once inside, she locked the door behind her and sat down on the closed lid of the toilet. She buried her face in her hands as tears welled up in her eyes.

Eli Stedford died in Solomon over twenty years ago...

How was that possible if he had moved to Bellville with his wife Nancy where she had then given birth to Paul? JoAnna knew the answer this question. She knew what Nancy had done. She leaned back against the toilet tank, looked up at the ceiling and drew the only conclusion that made any sense. This had to be the work of Isabelle Pearl. There was no other way. Isabelle must have returned Nancy Stedford's husband to her. The newspaper article in the book proved it. He had died in Solomon after only four short years of marriage to Nancy, and then died again, the second time by his own hand thirteen years later. Tears streamed down her face as JoAnna considered the prospects of this. But the article confirmed it, and coupled with Lydia's stories and the warning Sadie had given her, JoAnna realized that Wicked Izzy was real and obviously possessed an unspeakable power.

Lydia's words echoed through JoAnna's mind. *The price is different for each person...* If Nancy Stedford had gone to see Isabelle Pearl over the death of her husband Eli, what had she paid in return?

"What was her price?" JoAnna whispered to herself as she sat alone in the bathroom. She looked up at the ceiling and then down at her hands. What did Nancy give in return for thirteen more years with her husband? What had she lost? JoAnna searched her memories of Nancy trying to think of something. She tried to remember if Paul had ever said anything that might have offered a clue. But her mind only traveled in circles. She could not think of anything that Nancy could have given to Isabelle. Nothing Paul had ever said came to mind. Then her eyes grew wide, and she felt her heart flutter in her chest.

Paul... It was Paul. It had to be Paul. JoAnna drew in a sharp breath as the realization hit her. Was Nancy's price to lose her only child? She couldn't have known that at the time she made her deal with Isabelle. No mother would ever agree to such a thing. Lydia had said that a person never knows what the price is until it is time to pay, and only after Wicked Izzy had made good on her side of the bargain.

Hot tears rolled down JoAnna's cheeks. Nancy Stedford had visited Isabelle Pearl to have her husband returned to her, only to find out years later that her son would lose his life to settle her debt. The guilt had obviously been more than she could handle and as a result she had taken her own life. JoAnna considered all of this, and despite her misgivings she knew that she had to be right. Nancy had visited Isabelle Pearl and years later lost her only child because of it.

JoAnna leaned forward and rested her elbows on her knees again. The tears continued to come, steady droplets that fell to the floor at her feet. She finally had her answer, and she had found it in an old library in a town no one had ever heard of. Even though she had not been able to find any of Paul's relatives in town, she now understood the reason behind Nancy's secrecy about her past. She had made a deal with Wicked Izzy and in the process lost any chance to have life beyond her own. That was her price. It had to be. Nothing else made any sense. JoAnna settled on this for a moment. *No life beyond her own...* Her chin trembled as the tears traced warm paths down her cheeks.

No life beyond her own...

JoAnna remembered the night of the stillbirth when she and Paul had lost their child. She remembered the car skidding off the road in the storm and how Paul had to leave her on foot to go find help. She remembered being all alone while the ghost of Eli Stedford stood outside of the car pecking on the window with his dead, crooked finger.

JoAnna now realized that Nancy's price was to live alone in the world with no one to love her, with no bloodline to carry on. Not only did Wicked Izzy take Nancy's son Paul, she took her grandchild as well, thus ending her bloodline.

For a moment JoAnna thought she was going to vomit. She reached for the small trash can beside the sink but managed to fight off the nausea. Over a year's worth of pain and suffering was coming to the surface. Her heart ached for her husband, and their stillborn child. Then she heard Sadie approaching in the hallway, followed by a light knock on the door.

"Are you okay, dear?"

"I'm… I'm fine, Miss Sadie. I just needed to use the ladies' room. I'll be out in a second." She could see the shadow through the crack at the bottom of the door. Sadie was still standing in the hallway.

"Well, okay… I was just worried. I heard you run down the hallway and I just wanted to make sure you're okay."

"I'm fine," replied JoAnna, trying to mask the aggravation in her voice. She wished that Sadie would leave her alone. After a few more seconds, the shadow under the bottom of the door disappeared.

Suddenly the sound of JoAnna's cellphone broke the silence in the restroom. She flinched and quickly reached into her purse to retrieve the phone. She knew who it was even before she saw her mother's number on the screen.

"Yes, Mother," JoAnna replied, trying to speak as softly into the phone as she could.

"JoAnna Stedford, where are you and what are you doing? You didn't call to check in with me like you promised you would. What are you doing, young lady?"

"What am I doing? I'm sitting on the toilet in the Solomon public library, Mother. That's what I'm doing." JoAnna knew that sometimes the truth was the best option. "I'm trying to keep my voice down, okay?"

A long pause followed. "For some reason I believe you, JoAnna. Of all the lies a person could come up with I would think that wouldn't be one of them."

"I just checked on the car Mom and I saw the library across the street so I figured I'd kill some time."

"You sound like you've been crying. A mother can always tell."

JoAnna frowned into the phone, relieved that her mother couldn't see her face. "I'm fine, Mom. Really. I just miss you and I'm ready to come home, that's all. I'm ready to get out of here." JoAnna wiped her nose with a piece of tissue she pulled from a small box sitting on the edge of the sink. "I'm ready to finish my trip and come home."

"When will the car be ready?"

"They said maybe this afternoon. I promise I'll call as soon as I'm in the driver's seat again."

Maxine huffed into the phone. Her patience was wearing thin. She knew that her instincts about her daughter going on this foolish trip had been correct. Now she had a situation on her hands. Did she let her daughter continue to handle this on her own, or did she step in as her mother and fix the situation herself? Maxine knew the answer to the question but decided to let JoAnna think that she was going to continue to let her handle things all by herself.

"Okay then, JoAnna. But I promise you that if you are not on the road in the morning that I will come out there and get you myself."

"I promise, Mom. And if the car isn't ready by tomorrow morning, I won't fight you about it. If I'm not on the road in the morning, then I'll surrender and you can come get me." JoAnna closed her eyes and exhaled sharply. Deep down inside she knew her mother was right.

"Well, all right then, young lady. I love you. Call me first thing in the morning."

"I will, Mom. I love you too."

On the other end of the line standing alone in her kitchen, Maxine hung up the phone and stared at it sitting in the cradle on the wall. Then she walked to her bedroom, pulled a suitcase from her closet, and began to pack.

13

JoAnna collected herself for a few minutes after the call to her mother. When she looked in the mirror over the sink her appearance horrified her. She dabbed her red, puffy eyes with a tissue then reached into her purse for her hairbrush. As she stroked her hair, an idea surfaced in her mind. After a few more strokes, she tossed her hairbrush into her purse and left the restroom. Sadie peered over the top of her reading glasses at her as she approached the front desk.

"Miss Sadie, how many cemeteries are in Solomon?" Sadie looked at her as if she were speaking in a foreign language.

"I… I beg your pardon?"

"Cemeteries, Miss Sadie. How many are in Solomon?" JoAnna repeated, trying to hide her frustration.

Sadie paused for a moment. "Well… Just one, I suppose. Anyone who has ever died in this town is buried right down the road in the Solomon Memory Gardens. That's where my husband is buried."

JoAnna turned her head and looked out of the front window of the library. "Down that road?"

Sadie followed JoAnna's gaze to the front window. "Yes, right down that road you see out there, heading away from town. You go down about a quarter of a mile and you'll see a gravel road off to the right. There's a small sign. The cemetery sits in a large opening in the woods. There's even a small mausoleum, but last I heard was that it was just about full. Why do you ask?"

JoAnna knew she couldn't tell the woman the truth, but she decided she could at least tell her a lighter version of it.

"I saw a name in the book and I'd like to see if I can find the grave."

"What? Who? Whose name did you see?"

"It's a long story, Miss Sadie. I need to be going. I want to see if I can find the grave before it gets dark. Thank you for all your help."

Once outside JoAnna walked to the edge of the road and looked in the direction of the cemetery. In the distance, she could see the sign Sadie had mentioned. Then she looked in the other direction towards the main road through town and thought about Lydia and the diner. That would just have to wait. She knew that she had to find Eli Stedford's grave even if she had to check every tombstone in the cemetery. Seeing something in a book was one thing, but actually touching his headstone would help her to know if her theory was correct.

A narrow, grassy median separated each side of the road from the woods. After JoAnna had walked a minute or so, she crossed a wooden bridge over the swamp canal. She looked down into the black water and thought about how she had almost driven into it when she swerved to miss Eli's ghost standing in the road. Prickles rose on the back of her neck as she forced her eyes away from the water and back to the road ahead.

The thick woods on each side of the road heightened her feeling of isolation, and as much as she tried to avoid the thought, JoAnna realized that coming to the cemetery alone was probably a mistake. But she had to find Eli Stedford's grave. When she arrived at the sign, she stopped and looked down at it just as a crow cawed in the distance.

Solomon Memory Gardens. Established 1903

The sound of gravel crunching under her shoes echoed off the surrounding trees as she walked down the narrow road. She took the foot path to the cemetery and a feeling of dread washed over her when her hand touched the cold gate latch.

"It's too late to stop now," she whispered to herself as her hand worked against the rust holding the latch shut. A few more twists and a bump from her hip were all it took to get the gate open. Once through, she following a cobblestone path to the rear wall and the first row of tombstones. She had no idea where Eli was buried so her plan was to start at one end of the cemetery and move through each row until she found it.

The dates of death in the first row were in the early 1900s, with birthdates that predated the Civil War. Since these were some of the oldest graves in the cemetery, JoAnna knew Eli would not be in this section but just to make sure she turned and started up the next row. Sadie had said that this was Solomon's only cemetery. If Eli was here, she knew she would find him.

JoAnna pulled her sweater closed as a brisk wind combed through the headstones. Storm clouds were gathering overhead and she could feel the temperature dropping. Just as she was about to resume her search, a large crow landed on a headstone just a few feet away from her. It let out a loud *caw* and eyed her intently.

"Shoo! Get away from me!" She swatted at the crow but it only jumped along the headstones as she made her way down the row. When she got to the end of the row, it took flight and rejoined the other crows perched on the large statue sitting in the center of the cemetery.

By the time JoAnna made it to the center rows, the dates of death had risen into the 1970s and she knew she was getting close. Then out of the corner of her eye, she caught a movement off to her left. A man was walking alongside the wall on his way to a row of headstones carrying a handful flowers. He was old and moved with slow, deliberate motions. JoAnna watched as he turned and moved down one of the rows. When he found the grave he was looking for, he bent down and placed the flowers in the stone pot, then stood up and said a few words to himself. Once finished, he looked directly at JoAnna and tipped his hat before turning to make his way back to the gate.

The crows on the statue cawed in unison. JoAnna turned her attention away from the old man towards the crows and watched as more of them landed on the statue and the surrounding headstones. When she returned her attention to the old man, he was gone.

JoAnna brought her hands to her face and took a deep breath, trying to calm her nerves. She knew it was too late to stop now. She was hungry and figured her mind was just playing tricks on her, and that she had probably just imagined the old man. Perhaps his image was exactly what her mind had expected to see in a cemetery. She knew she had to keep going, had to keep searching because there wasn't much daylight left. Nothing mattered now except finding Eli's grave.

She stepped away from the fountain and after searching two more rows she stopped in front of a large tombstone shaped like a cross. She whispered the engraved words.

STEDFORD

Then she read the footstones.

Eli Wallace
Born August 3, 1959
Died September 9, 1986

Nancy Louise
Born March 23, 1960

JoAnna clinched her jaw and tried to fight back the tears. Panic cut through her abdomen as she read the words on the footstone. Unlike Eli's, Nancy's footstone carried no date of death. She remembered how Lynette had said that no one had come forward to take care of Nancy after she committed suicide. JoAnna realized that at that point there would have been no one left that knew about her grave plot here in Solomon. The county, just as it did with all unclaimed bodies, had cremated her and had probably buried her ashes in a grave somewhere near Bellville.

The weight of the truth pressed down on her as she stood at the foot of the grave of a man whose wife had made a deal with Wicked Izzy so that he could live again, a wife who had then paid a horrible price to square up that deal. JoAnna knew she had to be clinically insane for even considering the idea, but the proof was at her feet.

As JoAnna stared at footstones, things started to make sense to her. The book in the library, Eli's ghost in the road, Lydia's husband, and Sadie's warning. Now she understood everything. It was all true. The last hope that there had maybe been two people, both named Eli Stedford, and that this was all just a bizarre coincidence evaporated from her mind. Nancy's footstone was proof that the Eli Stedford buried in the grave in front of her was the same Eli Stedford that had killed himself in his own backyard shed, dying a second time long after the date engraved on the footstone at her feet.

JoAnna stepped backwards from the grave and looked around the cemetery. She had found what she was looking for and now realized that she needed to get back to town before the approaching storm arrived. She stepped into next row of tombstones, then turned and made her way down the row towards the cemetery wall. As she walked, she didn't pay much attention to the names on the stones until she got to the end of the row. She whispered the words engraved on the last stone in the row as the wind howled in the trees.

GREENFIELD

Raymond James
Corina Grace

Both names carried dates of death, with Corina's being about a year after Ray's.

Ray's been dead for three years... Lydia's words echoed through JoAnna's head as she stared blankly at the stone. With panic clawing at her insides, she broke and ran for the stone wall. Once she got to it, she turned and ran down its length until she came to the cemetery gate. She quickly darted through the gate and then through the trees until she was back on the gravel road that led to the main highway.

Just then Lydia's car skidded to a stop right in front of her.

14

Lydia jumped out of the car. "What in the hell are you doing out here, Jo? Are you crazy?"

JoAnna ran around the front of the car and grabbed Lydia and hugged her tightly. "Whoa," Lydia said as they embraced. "What's the matter, girl? Are you okay?"

"I found his grave, Lydia. I found Eli Stedford's grave." JoAnna felt the tears on her cheeks. "He's buried out there in that cemetery."

"Who? Eli who?" Lydia pushed JoAnna to arm's length so she could look into her eyes. "Who are you talking about?"

"It's him. I knew after seeing the article in the library book that I would find his grave in that cemetery." JoAnna wiped her eyes with the back of her hand. "It's all true."

"Okay Jo, you need to fess up. What haven't you told me? I thought we shared all our secrets about our husbands last night. Who is Eli? And what did you say his last name was?"

"Stedford," JoAnna replied. "Same last name as mine, same last name as his son, my husband. My dead husband…" A crack of thunder caused both women to jump, then the surrounding woods roared as the wind rushed through the tops of the trees. Dark clouds hung above them, bloated with rain.

"Let's get in the car, Jo. And then you're gonna tell me just what in the hell you're talking about." Just as they closed the doors, the downpour began. Within seconds it was raining so hard that neither of them could see through the windows.

Lydia looked at JoAnna sitting sheepishly in the passenger's seat. "I got worried when you didn't show up at the diner. I called Jared's garage and got Pike on the phone. He said you came in to check on the car and then walked across the street to the old library. Did you talk to Pike?" Lydia eyed JoAnna suspiciously, hoping that the answer was no.

"Not really…" JoAnna replied, wiping her eyes. "I mean, he was standing there when Jared was telling me about my car."

Lydia's eyes met JoAnna's. "Pike said he saw you come out of the library and walk down the street away from town. I knew at that point where you were going. You're lucky you didn't run into old Earl. He's Cooper's drinking buddy. They pay him to cut the grass out here every other week and I wouldn't want to be alone in an old lonesome cemetery with him around. Are you crazy? Why in the world did you come out here?"

JoAnna laid out the entire story of Eli, from what Paul had told her on their honeymoon about his suicide, right up to the point where his ghost had caused her to swerve off the road and almost drive into the swamp canal on her first night in town.

"It sounds like they lived here before I was born," Lydia said. "Like I told you, some people move away. Some move away because they know Wicked Izzy is evil, and some move away after they use her services because they think it will give them a new start. It's like they have this stupid idea that if they leave town, they won't have to pay the bill. That's what it sounds like this Stedford couple did. Sounds like this Nancy lady went to see Wicked Izzy and then left town with her husband after Izzy made good on their deal and returned him to her."

JoAnna nodded. "And then Nancy paid her price years later when Isabelle Pearl settled up with her."

"Time means nothing to Izzy. Everyone pays their price, Jo. Don't ever forget that." Lydia dropped her chin to her chest and began to turn the wedding band on her finger. "Everyone pays."

What JoAnna had found in the cemetery only proved to her that Nancy had visited Wicked Izzy after her husband died in the accident at the mill. But this still did not explain to her why the ghost of Eli Stedford was following her. Images of Eli haunting her dreams and of his apparition standing in the road flashed through her mind. Why was he haunting her? What did he want from her? JoAnna knew she had no part in what had gone on between Nancy and Isabelle Pearl. So why was Eli Stedford's ghost following her? JoAnna thought that maybe Lydia would be able to tell her why.

"It all makes sense now, Lydia, except that I don't know why Elis's ghost is following me. What does it want? I had nothing to do with what went on here in Solomon way back then. I wasn't even born when Nancy made her deal with Isabelle Pearl. Why won't he leave me alone?"

Lydia looked at JoAnna and then through the front windshield. The rain was so heavy that she could barely see the hood. She knew the answer to JoAnna's question.

"Sometimes Izzy chooses a servant, or maybe messenger is a better word for it." Lydia stared through the front windshield as if hypnotized by the falling rain. "She never leaves that house out there, never comes into town, never talks to anyone unless they want to make a deal. Sometimes I think she chooses a soul to do her bidding, to guide people to her. That could be what's going on now. This Eli person, maybe he's some sort of wayward soul, a servant of some sort. His soul, I mean. I've heard talk from people that have used Izzy's services. Every once in a while, you'll hear them talk about seeing ghosts."

Lydia and JoAnna locked eyes. "But remember, when a person makes a deal with Izzy, what she returns to them is not a ghost. When she brings someone back, they can be touched, felt... Loved... It's not some rotting corpse that claws its way out of the ground, or some ghost that can walk through walls or disappear into thin air." Lydia bowed her head and JoAnna watched a tear roll down her cheek. She sniffled and let out a hot breath. "What she brings back can be loved..."

Lydia paused for a few seconds before looking up at JoAnna. "Let me ask you a question, Jo. This Eli guy, you said he committed suicide when your husband was just a kid. Do you know where he was buried the second time he died?"

JoAnna remembered what Lynette had told her. "That neighbor I told you about, Lynette, she said Nancy had Eli cremated after he committed suicide." She wondered why Lydia would ask such a question.

"Cremation ends Izzy's spell. Or whatever it is, spell, magic, who knows. That tells me that you're not seeing the Eli that was returned to his wife. What you're seeing is his ghost, and if I had to guess, I'd say that Izzy sentenced his soul to roam this world in her service. Maybe now that you're here he'll consider his job done and move on to someone else. That is, if you go see Izzy. He probably won't leave you alone until you do. My guess is that he was sent here to make sure you visit her."

JoAnna looked at Lydia and then turned and tried to look out of the passenger side window. All she could see were thick sheets of rain hammering the ground around the car. She thought about what Lydia had just told her.

When she brings someone back, they can be touched, felt... Loved...
Loved...

JoAnna thought about Paul and how alone she felt without him. She thought about how empty her life was, and how no man would ever be able to fill the void he had left behind. What if she had him back? What if they had another chance? She thought about what Madam Valentine had said about Paul's soul, about how she could sense that he regrets the way things turned out and wants to be with her. And JoAnna thought about Lydia and how she had gone to see Isabelle. There were others too. Ray's wife had used Isabelle's services, and even though she didn't know much about Pike, she had her suspicions that he might also be Izzy's handiwork.

JoAnna thought about the price and how Lydia told her that eventually everyone pays. *So what?* she thought to herself. Just like Lydia, she had nothing left to lose. What could Isabelle possibly take from her? And what difference would it make as long as she could have Paul? They could run away together where no one would ever know the truth. The only person she would have to deal with would be her mother, and JoAnna knew she would think of something to handle that situation. She'd figure something out. The rest of their families were gone. Only her mother remained.

JoAnna realized that she had crossed some sort of boundary, a line between the rational and the irrational world. But she knew her choice was to either cross that line or spend the rest of her life alone. This realization was all it took for her to make up her mind. After a few seconds she turned and looked at Lydia, her eyes dark and carnal.

"Take me to her, Lydia. Take me to her right now."

15

Maxine leaned forward and tried to read the approaching road sign through the pouring rain. The hours on the road had dulled her senses, but she was able to make out the word *Solomon* and the number *3* as the sign glided past. A few minutes later she saw lights ahead and knew it had to be the town.

When she rolled past the first streetlight, she knew what she was seeing couldn't be Solomon. There were no signs of life anywhere, and as she rolled past the buildings, she was struck by the feeling that they looked abandoned instead of just closed for the night. But when she passed a sign that read *Lodging Ahead,* she felt her spirits rise.

"That's it," she said aloud as the wiper blades arced across the windshield. It had to be the motel JoAnna had told her about.

Maxine slowed down and turned into the gravel parking lot, reading the sign for the Swamp Fox Inn as she rolled past. When she brought the car to a stop, she stared through the front window at the thick sheets of pouring rain. All she could see was an abandoned motel with plywood nailed over all the windows. Astonished, she realized there was no way anyone had stayed at the motel in the last few days, or even the last few years. Why would her daughter lie to her?

She looked to her right and saw the dark outline of another building sitting on the edge of the motel's parking lot, close to the road. It too had boarded-up windows. A sign that read *Charlie's Diner* hung at an angle above the front entrance.

Anger flashed in her temples. Solomon was nothing more than a few abandoned buildings. What in the hell was going on? Why would her daughter tell her she stayed at the Swamp Fox Inn when it was a boarded-up and abandoned? And the diner was the same way. From what Maxine could see, the entire town of Solomon appeared completely abandoned. The only signs of life were the few streetlights placed along the road, each glowing with a faint, sickish light in the rainstorm.

Maxine decided it was time to call her daughter and find out just what in the hell was going on and why she had obviously turned into an unmitigated liar. Perhaps she needed to go back to the Morgan Institute for more therapy since anyone that could make up a story like this could not be of sound mind and body. With her hands trembling with anger, Maxine picked up her cellphone and prepared to dial JoAnna's number. When she saw that she didn't have a signal, she let out a stream of obscenities and threw the phone into the floorboard.

"This has got to be a damn mistake!" Maxine slapped the steering wheel as she looked at the dark box in front of her that used to be Charlie's Diner. She sat for a few moments unsure of what to do next and then decided to drive down the main road a few more miles to see what she could find. Maybe the diner she was looking at was the old one, and the owners had constructed a newer one farther down the road. Perhaps the Swamp Fox Inn had a new location as well.

She drove out onto the main road and made her way out of town as the heavy rain pelted her car. As the next sign approached, she squinted through the windshield in an effort to read the words.

East Pamlico Printing and Finishing.

Closed 1989.

Just as Maxine passed the sign, she saw an old gas station with boarded-up windows on the left-hand side of the road. Two ancient gas pumps sat in a circle of light thrown off by a nearby street light. There were no other lights around the building.

Just as Maxine brought her eyes back to the road ahead of her, she screamed and clamped down on the steering wheel. When her headlights hit the man standing in the middle of the road, she jerked the wheel to the right to avoid hitting him. Her foot found the brake pedal a moment too late and before she knew it, she was skidding down the grassy embankment towards the black water of the swamp canal.

Maxine screamed as the car left the embankment and crashed into the water. Terrified, her hands worked at the clasp on her seatbelt as the car sank into the water but she was unable to set herself free. Giving up on the latch, she flailed her arms about as panic engulfed her. She held her breath for as long as she could, then surrendered to the black water filling the car.

16

Lydia knew what JoAnna was getting herself into. She looked at JoAnna and turned the key in the ignition.

"This is your last chance to say no. If I take you all the way out there and leave you, there is no turning back. Once you step across the threshold of her door, you can't leave until the next morning. Izzy expects you to do all your thinking and hand wringing before you come to her. She assumes that once you show up on her doorstep that you know what you want and are willing pay for it."

JoAnna nodded. "My mind is made up, Lydia. I want Paul back. I've always wanted him back, but I had to know you were telling me the truth. The cemetery did it for me."

"I was the same way," Lydia said as she put the car in gear. "I'm crazy for that damn fool and I made my deal with Izzy. I just don't know what her price is yet, but I'm prepared to pay it. I miss him so much and I can't wait to hold him. He'll come back tonight just like he did the other night when you saw him outside my kitchen window. This time though, he'll stay."

JoAnna looked at Lydia and could see hope dancing in her eyes. The same feeling blossomed in her heart when she thought about touching Paul again. Then she caught herself when she realized that what she was thinking had to be the most outlandish idea she had ever considered. Yet deep down inside she knew it would come true. It had worked for other people, and now it would work for her.

Lydia turned the car around and started down the road away from town. She made a turn next to the abandoned barn and then picked up speed despite the pouring rain. Just as they crossed a small wooden bridge, she spoke.

"Her house is just up ahead."

Lydia clicked on her high beams to illuminate the road ahead. A few seconds later she slowed down and pulled over in front of a large, two-story farmhouse. JoAnna peered through the side window at the house and felt her nervousness ease. The yellow, incandescent light spilling from first-floor windows onto the porch created a warm and inviting feel, and portrayed an image exactly opposite of what she had expected to see. In her mind, she had pictured an old house with crows perched on the eves and an overgrown lawn in bad need of care. Izzy's house looked nothing like this.

"Listen Jo, there's one more thing I need to tell you. I should have told you before but, well, I just didn't know how."

JoAnna turned her attention away from the house to Lydia. She felt her nerves tighten.

"What is it?"

Lydia took a deep breath. "Izzy isn't always alone in her house. She has a son that comes around sometimes. Don't ask me where he comes from because I don't know. But sometimes he's in the house with her."

"What are you talking about, Lydia? What does her son have to do with anything?"

Lydia paused and looked past JoAnna at Izzy's house, remembering the night she spent there not too long ago. She looked at JoAnna with eyes full of compassion. She knew what the coming night held for her friend.

"Just drink the wine, okay? It's good, and it will help."

A puzzled looked crossed JoAnna's face. "Okay... I'll drink the wine. But what does her son have to do with anything?"

Lydia looked down into her lap for a few seconds and then back into JoAnna's eyes. "He has needs and I think Izzy likes for some of her houseguests to tend to those needs. Like I said, he's not in the house all the time, but he was when I stayed here. It... It wasn't... It wasn't bad, Jo. Nothing will go on in Izzy's house that you don't want to happen. Everything that happens will happen because you ask for it. Just be sure to drink the wine. It will make it easier for you. In fact, it will do more than that. It will make you... *needful.*"

JoAnna leaned against the passenger side door, stunned by what Lydia had just told her. She could see the sorrow in Lydia's face in the glow of the dashboard lights.

"Why didn't you tell me this earlier?"

"Would it have made any difference? Look at the bright side. Maybe young pretty girls like us have it easy with Izzy. You know, keep her son happy and that's the only price we have to pay. Wouldn't that be a kicker?" Lydia was trying to lighten the mood but JoAnna could see the doubt in her eyes. She knew Lydia didn't really believe this.

Lydia grinned. "He's a real looker too. Tall and strong... And he knows how to please a woman." Lydia fluttered a hand under her chin as if she was having a hot flash.

JoAnna reached over and squeezed her hand. "Hey, it's okay. I'm not mad at you for not telling me. And you're right. It wouldn't have made any difference. After what Paul's mother paid, I'd consider myself lucky if that's all Izzy wanted in return."

Lydia smiled weakly. "Like I said, Jo, I think he only comes around when a young woman spends the night in the house. Corina, Ray's wife, was in her seventies when she came to this house so I'm sure Izzy's son wasn't here when she spent the night. But she paid. I'm telling you that poor woman paid for having Ray back."

The blood drained out of JoAnna's face. "I'm afraid to ask. What was her price?"

"You don't wanna know."

"Tell me," snapped JoAnna. "What happened to her?" Lydia looked straight ahead through the foggy windshield, carefully choosing her next words.

"They lived out there in that old gas station on the edge of town. One night about a year after Ray returned, Corina just walked outside and stood by the edge of the road, then stepped in front of a semi hauling logs. It dragged her so far down the road that by the time the driver got the truck stopped there wasn't enough of Corina left to fill tea pitcher. They picked up what they could and buried it out there next to Ray's grave. No one knows why she did it. They say the poor old truck driver was crying like a baby when the sheriff showed up. He said she was wearing a nightgown and just stepped into his headlights before he could even hit the brakes."

"Noooo..." JoAnna whispered.

"Corina and Ray were good people. They lived above their gas station and had a picture of Jesus on the wall of every room. I think the guilt just got to her. She knew she had committed a sin. She knew it was wrong. That's my take on it, anyway. But Izzy kept up her end of the deal. She returned Ray and it lasted until Corina stepped in front of that truck. And now she's gone and Ray is the one left alone. I wish I could tell you how it all works but I just don't know. But I do know that if you make a deal with Izzy, she will keep her end of the bargain. You *will* get Paul back. And after that, well, you'll just have to take it one day at a time until you find out what she wants in return."

JoAnna looked at Lydia and then at Izzy's house, its front porch beckoning her in the pouring rain.

"It seems that the price is always death," JoAnna said, her voice laced with sarcasm. "Sometimes the innocent die too. If my theory is correct, my child was stillborn because of the deal Nancy made with Izzy. I should probably hate this woman. I don't know why I want to go in that house, but I just do."

"No," replied Lydia. "It's not always death. But sometimes when a person finds out what their price is, they just can't handle it and they commit suicide. Sort of like this Nancy lady. From what you've told me, she committed suicide over the guilt just like Corina did. They each paid Izzy in a different way but neither one of them could handle the guilt."

JoAnna considered this for a moment and then looked at Lydia just as a bolt of lightning electrified the air outside the car.

"I don't care what the price is because I won't be driven to suicide. Paul is worth it. And I don't care about Izzy's son, either. I'll give him whatever he wants if that's what it takes. Once I have Paul back, we're going to run away together and no one will ever know about any of this."

Lydia could see the fire in JoAnna's eyes, burning hot and lustful. She had told JoAnna everything she knew about Wicked Izzy and she still wanted to go in Izzy's house.

"Okay, then. I'll be here early tomorrow to pick you up." Lydia smiled as they hugged each other.

"Drink the wine," she whispered into JoAnna's ear before releasing her.

17

When JoAnna got to Isabelle's front porch, she stopped and collected herself. She wiped at her eyes to clear away the rainwater and then tried to peek through one of the windows. Just as she was about to knock on the front door, it swung open.

"Well hey there, JoAnna," Isabelle said with a smile. She was wearing a denim dress and an apron, and had long blonde hair that spilled onto her shoulders. The simple dress and the embroidered ducks on the apron completely dispelled the image JoAnna had anticipated. As ridiculous as it seemed now, in her mind she had expected to see an exotic sorceress with glowing eyes.

When JoAnna looked into Izzy's pale blue eyes she felt relief wash over her. *This is the witchy woman everyone in town thinks is so evil?* She thought about this for a few seconds, completely unnerved by Isabelle's beauty. *This is the woman that can recall a soul from the grave so that it can walk among the living?* Her mind raced as she compared the contrasting image of the real Isabelle Pearl with that of the raven-haired vamp she had expected to see. *This is the woman they call Wicked Izzy?*

Suddenly Isabelle closed her eyes and took a deep breath. "Mmmmm... Do you smell that?" When she opened her eyes, they shimmered with delight.

"I beg your pardon?" JoAnna replied.

"The fresh bread baking in my oven, silly." Isabelle beamed with pride as a pearly smile crossed her face. "Isn't it wonderful? I just love that smell, especially when it blends with the smell of the rain. It's just, well, *otherworldly*, don't you think? I always like to bake bread when it's raining outside." Suddenly she realized that she hadn't invited JoAnna into her house. "Oh, would you look at me. Where are my manners? Please come in."

JoAnna hesitated and then stepped through the door. Once in the foyer, Isabelle pushed the door shut and then turned and walked by JoAnna on her way to the kitchen. Then she stopped and turned around when she realized JoAnna wasn't following her.

"Let's go see how that bread is doing. I have sourwood honey and fresh butter just waiting for it to come out of the oven."

JoAnna took a step and stopped. "I don't mean to be rude, but how do you know my name?"

Isabelle smiled, her translucent blue eyes radiating patience and understanding, as well as a hint of amusement. "Bless your heart, sweetie," she said as she reached over and took JoAnna's hand. "I know everyone's name. I knew you were coming and I know why you're here. But we need to get to know each other before we go any further." Isabelle closed her eyes again and took in another long pull of the bread-scented air. "We can enjoy my bread while you tell me all about Paul."

JoAnna felt hope swell inside of her at the mention of Paul's name, then ashamed for being surprised that Isabelle already knew who she was. Isabelle released her hand then turned and walked towards the kitchen. The hardwood floor creaked as JoAnna followed her through the dining room. Incandescent light, warm and buttery, bathed walls decorated with framed embroidery. Once in the kitchen, Isabelle opened the oven door and removed two loaves of bread from the oven. She sat them on the stovetop and paused to sample the aroma again. She turned to JoAnna and grinned. "Just out of this world… Don't you think?"

"Yes, I do, Miss Pearl. The bread smells wonderful."

"Oh no you don't," replied Isabelle. "I'll have none of that Miss Pearl nonsense. Please call me Isabelle, or Izzy if you like."

JoAnna felt a flash of courage. "People in town call you…" she said before losing her nerve.

A mischievous grin crossed Isabelle's face. "I know, sweetie. They call me Wicked Izzy. Can you imagine?" She tilted her head and placed her hands on her hips, feigning disbelief. "Now I ask you, do I look wicked standing here in my duck apron?"

"Well, Miss… I mean, Isabelle, to be honest I wasn't expecting you to look like you do. I guess I don't really know what I was expecting. My friend Lydia said you were a very beautiful woman, but she didn't really describe you. I did see a picture of you in a book in the library, but it wasn't a close-up photo." JoAnna thought about the old photo and how young Isabelle looked in it. She reminded herself that she was talking to a woman who apparently had not aged over the decades. She wanted to ask about this but decided it would be rude given that they were just getting acquainted. Despite Isabelle's Southern charm, JoAnna tried to remember who she was talking to. An image of the tombstones in the cemetery flashed through her mind.

"Lydia… Yes, such a sweet girl. How's she doing?"

"I think she's doing okay. She was very nice to me and let me stay with her last night. I was afraid of that old motel in town and the guy that works there. I spent my first night in one of the rooms and it was pretty scary."

Isabelle narrowed her eyes. "You must be talking about Cooper."

JoAnna nodded. "He's the night man."

"I know who he is, and I have something planned for him. He won't be bothering anyone much longer."

Suddenly JoAnna felt sympathy for Cooper, even though he had scared her. She got the feeling that Isabelle Pearl, despite her Southern charm, was probably the last person someone would want for an enemy.

"Well, yes, he was scary," JoAnna continued. "Lydia let me stay with her during my second night in town so I didn't have to see him again." She looked over at the small kitchen table that looked like something out of the 1950s and Isabelle took the cue immediately.

"Have a seat," she said, motioning at the table. "I'll get the honey and butter. So, Jared has your car. How is that going?"

"It's going well. I think he has a mechanic named Pike working on it." JoAnna sat down and ran her hand over the surface of the old kitchen table.

"Pike…" Isabelle flipped a pan over onto a towel, releasing the warm bread.

"Pike is Emma's fiancé. I don't believe you've met her, have you?"

JoAnna frowned, "No, I haven't met anyone named Emma yet."

Isabelle nodded. "Pike died too soon and Emma just couldn't bear it. She was so sad. She's the type of girl that I just love to help."

JoAnna thought about Pike's dark eyes and how they reminded her of Ray's. Isabelle brought a loaf of bread over to the table and then retrieved two small plates and a jar of honey.

"Emma is a sweet girl, but she's not as sweet as you are, JoAnna. I have very special plans for you. I've been waiting for you for a long time and was beginning to think you might not come."

"I'm not sure I really had a choice," JoAnna said as she looked down into her lap. Then she looked at Isabelle again. "Did you send him to make sure I made it to Solomon, and to this house?" She didn't want to offend Isabelle, but she needed to know if Lydia's theory about Eli was correct.

"You're very smart, JoAnna. That's one reason I have such special plans for you." Isabelle took a knife and cut a slice of bread. She laid it on JoAnna's plate before cutting a slice for herself. When her eyes met JoAnna's, they were the color of faded denim.

"Did he help you?" JoAnna said, regaining her composure as she buttered her bread. She followed with a dollop of honey.

"Let's just say I was owed a favor," Isabelle said as she smoothed honey onto her slice of bread. "But now that you're here, I suspect that you won't be seeing him anymore." She raised the bread to her lips and took a bite. "Mmmmm… So delicious…"

JoAnna couldn't resist any longer and took a bite of her bread. The sweet honey and butter combined with the warm bread ignited a wave of pleasure that she could feel all the way to her toes. Before she knew it, she had eaten the entire piece.

When Isabelle realized she had forgotten the wine, she sat her piece of bread down on her plate and frowned. "What is wrong with me today?" She got up from the table and returned with a carafe of wine, then cut another slice of bread and placed it on JoAnna's plate "I make the wine myself," she said before retrieving two glasses from the cupboard.

"You make it yourself?" JoAnna eyed the carafe with suspicion. Something told her the wine was going to be hard to swallow. She knew she liked homemade whiskey, Lydia had showed her that, but homemade wine was another story. She wasn't even a fan of wine sold in stores, much less wine made in someone's kitchen.

Isabelle winked a blue eye. "It's strawberry. I grow them myself right out there in my garden. You'll love it."

After hearing her comment about Cooper, the last thing JoAnna wanted to do was offend the woman. She reached for the glass and took a sip, expecting the worst. But the wine had a smooth and sugary taste that she found delightful, so much so that she immediately took another sip. "This is delicious," she said, smacking her lips together. Then she put her hand over her mouth in embarrassment. "Excuse my manners." she said, smiling shyly. "Do you really make it yourself?"

"I do," Isabelle said as she took another bite of bread.

"Paul made homemade wine once from a recipe he got from some guy he worked with. It was just after we bought our house in Charleston. We both took a sip of it and decided we'd rather drink from the toilet." JoAnna giggled as the memory of Paul's rancid wine came back to her. After just two sips of Isabelle's wine, she could already feel herself loosening up. She reached for her cup and took a third sip, relishing the taste as it slid easily down her throat. Then she looked into Isabelle's eyes.

"I really miss him. He was everything in the world to me and I'd give anything to have him back. Anything... I wanted to have children and grow old together. But I guess it just wasn't meant to be." She gazed into Isabelle's eyes, glowing soft and blue with compassion.

"I can help you JoAnna, but I need to ask you a question first." Isabelle took the carafe and topped off both of their cups. JoAnna took a sip and had to fight the urge to finish the entire cup all at once. She could feel the heat rising in her cheeks from the alcohol.

"Okay, you can ask me anything, Isabelle."

"Did Lydia tell you that before I can help someone, they must be alone in this world?"

JoAnna looked down at her cup and searched her memory. "Lydia told me her parents died in a car wreck, leaving her all alone. And she said something about her grandparents being gone too. But I'm not alone, Isabelle. I have my mother. Everyone else in my family is gone but I still have her." JoAnna felt a pang of disappointment at the idea that Isabelle might not be able to help her since she wasn't alone, then a weak smile crossed her face. "But I am alone when it comes to men. If that... If that matters. I haven't been with another man since I lost Paul. In fact, I've never been with any man except him."

Isabelle smiled. "Your love is so pure, JoAnna. That is all I require. Sometimes people come to me over a lost loved one and I realize their grief is not deep enough and that it will pass if just given time. These are the ones I turn away. I can only help those that feel like they cannot go on without my help. Their grief must be overwhelming. My power comes from the same dark place as their grief, and it is very strong."

Hope blossomed in JoAnna's heart. "I don't have to be alone?"

"No, you do not," Isabelle replied, lying to JoAnna. She knew she could only help a person who was alone, but it was not necessary for the person to know this.

JoAnna let out a sigh of relief. She took another long drink of her wine and felt her head swim with delight.

"I'm so relieved, Isabelle. I thought for a minute you were going to tell me that you couldn't help me because my mother is still alive. I love her very much even though until just recently we hardly ever got along. But I do love her. She is all I have left. My father has passed and so have all of my grandparents."

"You don't have to be alone," Isabelle said as she emptied the carafe into their cups. Then she got up and retrieved another one from the pantry and sat back down at the table.

"Lydia had no one left in this world when she came to me. But that wasn't a requirement. And soon she will be reunited with her husband."

JoAnna felt her entire body hum with excitement. Now there were no barriers to Isabelle's help. She grabbed her cup and took a long sip of the sweet wine and felt every nerve ending in her body sing with joy. Lydia had been right about the wine. It was very good, and JoAnna knew that without it, things would be much more difficult. It would be hard to have a conversation about waking the dead without alcohol to blur the lines of reality.

"May I ask you one more question?" Isabelle said as she took another sip of her wine. JoAnna followed suit, unable to resist the taste of the delicious elixir.

"Yes, you may."

Isabelle's eyes settled on her cup and then rose to meet JoAnna's. "Do you want me to help you? You must say so of your own free will. I cannot, and will not, force you to do anything. If you stay the night, it must be of your own free will. And whatever happens here tonight will happen because you want it to happen."

Isabelle's Southern drawl was soft and bewitching but JoAnna still felt apprehensive. She took another sip of wine and felt desire stir deep inside her. She looked into Isabelle's eyes, then spoke the words that would change her life forever.

"I want your help, Isabelle. Return Paul to me and I will do anything you ask in return."

18

Outside the storm grew more intense. Bright flashes of lightning lit the landscape around Isabelle's house as the wind blew the rain against the windows and thunder rumbled in the distance. Isabelle and JoAnna were sitting at the kitchen table finishing off their second carafe of strawberry wine. The wine was having no effect on Isabelle but was causing every fiber of JoAnna's body to burn with anticipation.

"Lydia told me about how everyone has to pay a price for your help." The wine was loosening JoAnna's inhibitions, causing her to lose her fear of asking questions.

"I do require something in return, JoAnna. But I won't tell you what it is. You must be willing to take the next step only with the knowledge that there will be a day of reckoning. And you must understand that your day of reckoning may come tomorrow or it may come years from now. I'm a very patient woman. Sometimes I wait for years before I demand payment."

JoAnna's eyes widened and her voice dropped to a whisper. "Do I… Do I have to die?"

Isabelle's eyes lit up with surprise. "Of course not, silly. No, you don't have to die. It's not like I exchange one soul for another."

JoAnna didn't think such an enchanting woman would lie to her, but a tiny flicker of doubt remained. "But some of the others…" She moved her cup in small circles on the tabletop. "It seems that was the price for some of the people Lydia told me about. Ray's wife Corina, Lydia said she stepped in front of a truck."

"That was not my doing. Corina found out what I wanted in return for helping her and when we settled our bargain, she couldn't live with it. But I did not ask for her soul in return for Ray's."

"What did you ask for?"

"I asked only for her memories of him, for the sixty years of love burning in her heart. She gave it to me and he became a stranger to her. She couldn't handle it so she ended her life." Isabelle's eyes flickered with contentment as she recalled her deal with Corina.

"Will you ask that of me? Will you return Paul to me only to turn him into a stranger, into someone I feel like I've never met before?"

Isabelle's tone softened. "Of course not, but I will not tell you what I want from you. You must be prepared to take the chance, to not know what your day of reckoning will bring. Call it, well, call it a leap of faith."

JoAnna pushed her empty wine cup away and felt a steely resolve rush through her body. This was her chance.

"I can't go on without him so take whatever you want from me. I'll pay any price."

A ghost of a smile crossed Isabelle's face. "Then we have a deal, JoAnna. Come with me."

"Before we go can I ask you one more question? I promise it's my last."

Isabelle settled back into her chair. "Of course, but I already know what you're going to ask."

"You do?"

"You want to know about your child, why he was stillborn."

JoAnna hesitated, then gathered what courage she could muster against the effects of the wine. "Why did I have to lose my child?"

Isabelle placed her hand on JoAnna's. "Nancy's price was that her bloodline end with her."

JoAnna thought about this and frowned. "But she gave birth to Paul after she made the deal with you. How could that happen if her bloodline had to end?"

"I allowed that to happen because of you."

"Because of me?" JoAnna tried to focus her eyes but the wine made it difficult. Suddenly the kitchen table stretched and yawed in front of her. She grasped the edge of it to steady herself.

"I allowed Nancy to have Paul because I knew it would one day lead you to me. Like I said JoAnna, you are a special girl. I've been waiting for you for a very long time. Now, shall we go?"

Isabelle rose from the kitchen table and extended her hand.

JoAnna hesitated, but then reached out. Once on her feet, she swayed and caught herself on the edge of the table with one hand while holding Isabelle's hand with the other.

"Where are we going?" JoAnna asked as the room tilted. She squeezed Isabelle's hand for support.

"You must stay the night, JoAnna, in my attic bedroom. The bed is old but very inviting. You must sleep underneath the hand-sewn quilt and you cannot leave until the sun rises in the morning. Do you understand?" JoAnna looked at Isabelle, who seemed to split into two images before combining back into one.

"That's... That's it? That's all I have to do?"

"No, there is more," Isabelle said as they moved away from the table and out of the kitchen. She led JoAnna through the dining room and up the stairs. Once at the top, they moved down the hallway until they were standing in front of the door leading to the attic bedroom.

"Your bedroom is at the top of the stairs."

"I... I understand. You said there is more, can you tell me what it is? What else do I have to do?"

Isabelle's blue eyes shimmered in the dim light of the hallway. "Sweet girl... You are so very special," she said as she cupped JoAnna's face in her hands. "You will find everything you need in the bedroom above. There are night clothes in the dresser if you choose to wear them. And remember, you must sleep in the bed under the quilt.".

"But I thought you said there was... You said..."

Isabelle placed a finger on JoAnna's lips. "I've told you all I can for now," she said as she opened the door revealing a narrow, dimly lit staircase leading to the attic bedroom.

JoAnna turned to Isabelle but could tell by the look in the woman's eyes that she had nothing more to say. She turned to the staircase and after a few steps heard Isabelle close the door behind her. Once at the top of the stairs she turned and looked down at the hallway door. There was no turning back now. She closed her eyes for a moment, opened the door and stepped into the room.

Once inside, she surveyed the room. A small, ornate crystal lamp sat on a nightstand next to the bed, its weak light fighting against the shadows. When she sat down on the edge of the bed, she noticed the intricate carvings covering the headboard. She traced the edge of one of them with her finger and then ran her hand across the quilt covering the bed, remembering Isabelle's instructions about sleeping under it.

The earlier dizziness from the wine had receded, replaced by a strange feeling of needfulness and desire. She wanted to get out of her clothes and into the bed where she could curl up and think about having Paul again. Maybe tomorrow night he would be in the bed with her. Maybe tomorrow night she would feel his hands on her body, his warmth soothing her as he held her close. Isabelle had not told her how long it would take for Paul to return, but she hoped it would be soon.

JoAnna stood up and walked to the dresser, pulled open the top drawer and found the nightclothes Isabelle had mentioned. Once out of her clothes and in the nightgown, she crawled under the quilt and within minutes was fast asleep.

Sometime around midnight her eyes fluttered open. Disoriented and unable to remember where she was at, she sat up on her elbows just as a flash of lightening lit the room's lone window and momentarily scalded the walls a brilliant white. She gasped when she saw the outline of someone standing in front of the window.

"Isabelle…? Isabelle, is that you?" JoAnna's heart thumped in her chest as she strained to focus on the outline of the woman. "Isabelle?" she said again. "Why are you in my room?" There was still no answer from the dark figure standing in front of the window.

The woman walked across the room towards the bed. JoAnna pulled the edge of the quilt closer to her face but was too scared to get out of the bed and run for the door. When she managed to find the courage to reach over and turn on the lamp, the dim light revealed the woman's face.

JoAnna gasped, barely able to speak. "Mom? Is that you? What are you doing here? You scared me to death! How did you find me?"

JoAnna got out of bed, grabbed her mother and hugged her. Maxine raised her arms and put them around her daughter, then JoAnna pushed her away so that she could get a good look at her face.

"Mom, you're wet. Why are you wet? Did you drive all the way here from Spartanburg?" Maxine stared into JoAnna's eyes as if she couldn't hear her, then she raised her hands and placed them on her daughter's cheeks.

"Oh, JoAnna… I love you so much, sweetie." Her eyes softened as she looked at her daughter.

"I… I love you too, Mom," JoAnna said, surprised by the words. "What's going on?"

Fear filled Maxine's eyes. "Get out of this house, JoAnna. Get away from her. She's evil. She only appears to you the way you want her to appear. You don't want what she has to offer." Maxine's hands felt cold and clammy. JoAnna reached for them and pulled them from her face. Something was wrong with her mother.

"Get out of this house, JoAnna. Get out while you still can."

Maxine's eyes turned dark and her breathing faltered. She took a step backwards and put her hand over her mouth. A cough rattled in her chest, then she spit a mouthful of dark swamp water into her hand.

"I'm so sorry, JoAnna," she said in a hoarse growl. She raised her arms to reach for her daughter and then faded away. This was more than JoAnna could take. She felt her head swim, then she fell backwards on the bed and passed out.

An hour later her eyes fluttered open. She gasped, sat up in the bed and called out her mother's name again, then slid off the bed and stumbled across the room to the bathroom door. Once back in bed, she convinced herself that her mother's appearance had only been a nightmare and within minutes was fast asleep.

JoAnna didn't hear the bedroom door open, despite the squeaking of the old hinges, and she didn't hear the young man as he stepped into the room and closed the door behind him. The old floorboards creaked as he walked across the room and when he pulled the quilt away from her face, her eyes opened.

"Paul?" she said, her voice heavy with sleep. The young man remained silent. "Is that you?"

The young man placed a finger across her lips and then traced it along her cheek. His touch was warm and inviting and she made no effort to push him away.

"I am not Paul," the young man said as he moved his hand down her body, enjoying the feel of her skin underneath the soft nightgown. His touch ignited a firestorm of desire deep inside her. The dizziness from the wine was gone, replaced by carnal desire.

"*Take me…*" she whispered.

19

JoAnna woke to the yellow light of dawn sifting through the bedroom window drapes. She sat up in bed, unsure of where she was at, and when she did a bolt of pain shot through her head. She immediately collapsed back onto the mattress. The pounding in her head pulsed in tune with the beat of her heart. Then a hazy memory of the young man visiting her in the night surfaced in her mind. She looked around the room, then brought a hand to her face and exhaled through her fingers.

What have you done, JoAnna Stedford?

Her head throbbed in protest as she slid out from underneath the quilt and walked to the bathroom. Once finished, she came back to the bed and removed the nightgown. She dressed quickly and then sat on the edge of the bed staring at the closed door, unsure of what to do next. Then she looked again at the window and the dawn light streaming through the drapes.

You must not leave until the sun rises...

JoAnna remembered the horrible nightmare about her mother. She knew she needed to call her mother but one look at the nightstand and the absence of her purse told her that the call would have to wait. Then she remembered what Lydia had told her about Isabelle's son and how he was sometimes in the house. Her cheeks warmed as the previous night's encounter started coming back to her. She took a deep breath and exhaled slowly. *So be it,* she thought. There was nothing she could do about it now.

After she came to grips with the fact that she had given herself to a stranger during the night, she thought back to the earlier events of the evening. She remembered making a deal with Isabelle, agreeing to pay her price in exchange for having Paul returned to her. A smirk crossed her lips as she thought about how ridiculous that sounded. Her husband was dead and had been for over a year.

JoAnna stood up and took a deep, cleansing breath. It was time to go downstairs. For better or worse it was time to see what was going to happen. She walked across the bedroom until she was standing at the door that led downstairs. With more courage than she ever knew she could muster, she reached out and opened the door.

Once down the stairs, she stopped again before opening the door to the hallway. She needed a moment to collect herself and to prepare for what might be on the other side. When she opened the door, the smell of bacon greeted her, along with the sound of Isabelle singing to herself in the kitchen below.

JoAnna thought about Paul. What if he was sitting at the kitchen table waiting for her? Could it be as simple as that? Surely not… Excitement fluttered in her chest at the thought of being reunited with her husband, and this quickened her steps as she moved down the hallway towards the stairs to the first floor. Once at the bottom she turned and walked into the kitchen, afraid of what, or who, she might see.

Isabelle was standing in front of the stove frying bacon in a cast-iron skillet. Her dress was different from the night before but she had on the same duck apron. She was poking at the bacon in the skillet when she suddenly sensed JoAnna's presence.

"Well good morning, sleepyhead," she said. "The coffee is right over there. I don't know about you, but I'm just the devil until I have my first cup."

"Is he here?" JoAnna said, ignoring the coffee pot. "I thought…"

"Oh sweetie, it just doesn't work like that. You didn't think he'd be sitting at the table waiting for you, did you? But don't worry. You'll see him soon enough. Now be a good girl and have a cup of coffee, then we'll talk about it."

JoAnna looked warily around the kitchen. They were alone. "I'm a bear too until I have my first cup. Sometimes it takes two, to tell you the truth." She walked over and poured herself a cup, then added cream and lots of sugar. Isabelle raised an eyebrow as she watched.

"I knew you liked it sweet. You just seem like that kind of girl." Isabelle took a fork and removed the bacon, then emptied a bowl of chopped potatoes, onions and green peppers into the skillet. A loud hissing noise followed. "You do like home fries, don't you?" she said with a grin.

"They're my…" JoAnna caught herself before she finished.

"They're your favorite, I know," Isabelle said as she stirred the mixture with a wooden spatula. JoAnna noticed she wasn't using a mitt to hold the hot handle of the skillet.

JoAnna raised her cup to her lips and took a long sip of coffee. A wave of pleasure rushed through her senses as the hot liquid went down her throat. After another sip, she looked at Isabelle standing in front of the stove.

"How… I mean, what happens next?"

Isabelle turned and looked at JoAnna. "Let's eat first and then we'll discuss the details. I insist."

JoAnna picked up on Isabelle's tone and knew not to ask again. She nodded towards the table. "May I?"

"Of course, sweetie."

Once finished with the home fries, Isabelle scrambled eggs in another pan and then placed all the food on the table, smiling proudly. "Help yourself."

JoAnna scooped eggs onto her plate, along with home fries and a few slices of bacon. After several bites, she dabbed her mouth with her napkin and then looked at Isabelle sheepishly.

"I don't mean to be a bother. But, well, last night… A young man was in my room. I remember him touching me and I remember, well…" JoAnna looked down into her lap as she felt her cheeks warm. "It's just that, I mean, I'm so embarrassed. We did something, something I haven't done in a long time, and, well, something I've never done with anyone except Paul."

"Did he hurt you? Did he do anything against your will?" Isabelle said as she placed her hand on JoAnna's.

"Oh no, not at all," JoAnna said as her eyes fell to her lap again. "No, he didn't hurt me. In fact, it was… It was nothing like that at all. I remember that I didn't want him to stop." She exhaled sharply. "I don't know what came over me." She raised her chin and looked into Isabelle's pastel-blue eyes.

"He's my son, JoAnna. He wasn't there to hurt you. Don't you know I'd take a switch to that boy if I found out that he hurt you? You're very special and I will not allow any harm to come to you, even after you leave my house."

"Your son? Then Lydia was right." JoAnna let her eyes drift to the kitchen window, illuminated by the soft glow of early morning light. "Lydia told me that sometimes your son is in the house."

"He lives here, but he stays gone a lot. You know how young people are," Isabelle said as she rolled her eyes. "But you won't see him again, and no one needs to know what went on in your room last night. We all have our secrets, you know." Isabelle winked and then took a long sip of her coffee.

JoAnna wondered again how anyone could call this woman *Wicked Izzy* when she seemed so homespun and polite. Then she thought about the tombstones in the cemetery and the stories around town.

"Paul… Can you tell me about Paul? When will I see him?" JoAnna blurted out the words before she could stop herself. "You and I have an agreement, Isabelle. What happens now?"

Isabelle took a sip of coffee and then sat her cup down on the table. "You must journey to the place where he left this world. He will return to you there. It is at this place where I will make good on our deal. It is there where he will begin his second life."

"How can I…?" JoAnna stammered. This meant she had to return to their house in Charleston. But she remembered her mother telling her that the bank had foreclosed on it while she was in therapy after Paul's suicide. Surely someone else was living in it by now.

"You will find a way." Isabelle cupped her hands around her coffee cup and looked at JoAnna. "I can promise you that you will find a way. When you do, he will be there waiting for you. I don't go back on my word, JoAnna. A deal is a deal. Travel to the place where he took his life and you will find him waiting for you. This is how I will make good on my end of our bargain. And then when the time comes, you will make good on your end."

JoAnna felt her throat tighten. She didn't want to discuss the price she had to pay. Maybe it was better not to know.

"What about my car?"

Isabelle's eyes lit up. "I have a surprise for you. Come see."

Isabelle stood up and walked out of the kitchen, through the dining room and to the front door. JoAnna followed. Once at the door, Isabelle opened it and stepped onto the front porch. "Pike brought it to my house early this morning," she said as she waved an arm at the red Mercedes sitting in the driveway.

"You're kidding!" exclaimed JoAnna. "How did you manage

that?" she said, suddenly realizing what a foolish question that was. She knew Isabelle Pearl had a way of getting things done.

A mischievous grin crossed Isabelle's face. "Let's just say he owes me a favor, like most people in town. That's some kind of red, don't you think?"

JoAnna suddenly remembered Danny at the gas station she stopped at on her way to Solomon. He had used the exact words to describe her car, right before he warned her to stay on the main road through the swamps. Could he have known about Isabelle? Was he another example of her work?

"I discussed the bill with Jared and it's taken care of. He followed Pike out so that he could give him a ride back to town."

"I don't know what to say, Isabelle. It had to have cost hundreds of dollars."

"It didn't cost a cent, sweetie. Don't even worry about that." Isabelle paused, then winked at JoAnna. "That Pike is such a sweet boy, especially the second time around."

JoAnna felt her spirits rise. Her car was in the driveway ready to take her out of Solomon. The only thing she had to worry about now was calling her mother, but at least she would be able to report that the car was ready to go. She turned and looked at Isabelle. "Thank you again. I'll get my purse and I guess I'll be on my way. I need to go by Lydia's and get my other bag."

Isabelle smiled but said nothing. JoAnna disappeared into the house and returned a few moments later with her purse. "Thank you again for everything," she said as she gave Isabelle a hug.

When they parted, Isabelle said, "you will thank me when the time comes, JoAnna. Remember that."

20

When JoAnna pulled into the gravel lot of Jared's garage, she saw a *CLOSED* sign hanging in the window of the office door. Then she remembered Miss Sadie. She turned and looked over her shoulder at the library and decided that she should at least say goodbye to her.

Once inside the library, JoAnna looked around and to her surprise saw a young girl with a shock of red hair sitting behind Miss Sadie's desk.

"Can I help you?" asked the girl.

"Um... Yes," JoAnna said as she walked across to the girl's desk. "I just wanted to see..."

Just as she was about to ask about Miss Sadie, JoAnna looked at the row of photos hanging on the wall. On the left end of the row was a photo of Miss Sadie that had not been there yesterday. To the right of her photo were the photos of the other women, the ones Miss Sadie had told her were past librarians. The young girl behind the desk sensed her confusion and tried to help.

"It's our own librarian hall of fame. They're all gone now. The one on the end is Miss Sadie. She trained me right before she died. Such a sweet lady... Everybody in town just loved her. I guess one day my photo will be up there next to hers." The young girl paused and looked at JoAnna.

"Is there something I can help you find?"

After a few seconds, JoAnna finally managed to mutter a few words.

"But I... I was..." Her words dropped off and her eyes returned to the photo. The young girl could tell something was wrong so she tried to make small talk to ease the silence.

"I'm happy to be back at work today. I was out yesterday with an upset stomach. That'll teach me to eat at Charlie's diner. There's no telling what kind of meat that is in his chili." The girl stuck out her tongue and crinkled her nose.

JoAnna ignored the joke about the chili. "Do you mind if I ask you when Miss Sadie passed away?"

The girl frowned as she thought about it. "Oh, I guess it's been going on five years now. She was so sweet. But she was alone. Her husband died a long time ago at the mill and she never remarried. Such a lonely life... The library was all she really had, and she looked over it like it was her child."

JoAnna felt her stomach roll. Images of Isabelle Pearl flashed through her mind. Surely Miss Sadie wasn't... She quickly forced the thought out of her mind.

The girl continued, eager to tell the story. "Like I said, she was alone. She lived right upstairs and took care of the library for a long time. She died one night in her sleep right upstairs in her bedroom. They offered to let me live here too, but I said no. I mean, that's just too creepy. Besides, I live with my boyfriend. We're getting married." The young girl leaned back in her chair as a triumphant grin spread across her face.

"Five years?" JoAnna felt her knees wobble. She looked at the young girl and waited for her to confirm this again.

"Yep. I'd say it's been about five years. She's buried right down the road in our cemetery."

JoAnna had heard enough. Surely Miss Sadie wasn't more of Isabelle Pearl's handiwork. She couldn't have been. Her eyes... They were not like Pike's and Ray's. They were clear and full of compassion. But if Miss Sadie wasn't more of Isabelle's handiwork, how had she been in the library yesterday?

"I need to be going," JoAnna said as she looked at the girl and then back at the photo of Miss Sadie. "Thank you for your help."

"Um, sure. Not that I really helped you. But come on back if you change your mind and want to check out a book. My name's Emma and I'm here all day."

Emma... JoAnna forced a smile, then turned and walked to the front door. Once outside she took a deep breath and tried to gather her nerves. Solomon was getting stranger by the minute. She walked back to the car and felt a chill run down her spine when the wind rushed through the trees behind Jared's garage. Once back in her car, she locked the doors but it did little to ease her apprehension.

When she looked over at her purse sitting in the passenger's seat, she remembered that she needed to call her mother. After taking one more look around to be sure no one was walking up on her, she reached into her purse and retrieved her phone. She pushed the button for her mother's number and waited for an answer. After about ten rings she pulled the phone away from her ear, stared at it in disbelief and then ended the call.

"Where are you, mother?" she whispered as she dropped the phone back into her purse. She put the car in gear and pulled out of the parking lot of the garage. In a few seconds she was back on the road headed towards the diner. When she pulled into the parking lot, she didn't see Lydia's car, and when she looked across at the Swamp Fox Inn she saw charred brick around the office door. Had the office caught fire last night? The rest of the building looked unscathed. She pulled the car closer to the office but couldn't find the courage to get out for a closer look. Then she thought about Cooper. Maybe she could ask about him in the diner.

"Table for one? There's a booth by the window, or you can sit at the counter if you like," the server said as JoAnna walked into the diner. Instead of taking a booth, she stepped up to the counter and took a seat on a stool.

"Do you mind if I ask you a question?"

"Shoot," replied the server, eager to help.

"What happened to the Swamp Fox Inn?"

"Oh, it was terrible. It caught fire last night. The fire department thinks it was Cooper's old coffee pot that started it. He slept in the back room right off of the office, you know. It was so sad… But they got here before the whole thing burned down. The fire didn't spread much past the office."

"Sad?" JoAnna said.

"Poor old Cooper. He didn't make it. Nobody really liked him, but no one wanted to see him burn up like that. It was just terrible. Charlie saw the whole thing. He's the one that called the fire department."

She took in a deep breath. "Cooper is dead?"

"Yep. The fire got him. Like I said, he was a weirdo but nobody deserves to go out like that."

"That's terrible," JoAnna said. "I stayed at the Swamp Fox a few nights ago. Cooper was a little on the strange side but I hate to think of him being burned alive." She felt a shiver run through her body as she remembered Isabelle's words.

I have something planned for him...

The server eyed JoAnna. "Are you okay?"

"Um... yes, I'm fine," replied JoAnna, trying to fight back the tears. Her words to Isabelle had caused another human being to lose his life.

"Are you sure you're okay?" the server asked again. She stopped rolling her silverware and stared at JoAnna.

"I'm... I'm okay."

"Table for one, then?"

"Actually, I'm just looking for Lydia. Is she working today?"

"She's supposed to be here," she said as she put down the silverware and picked up a menu hoping that JoAnna would place an order.

"She didn't come to work?"

"Nope. She's a no show today. That's why I'm here. Today is my day off, but Charlie called me in when Lydia didn't show up this morning. If you see her, tell her to get her butt in here so I can go home."

"Well, I know where she lives. I'll just ride out to her trailer and see if she's there."

"Like I said, tell her to get her butt in here and that Charlie's pissed off."

JoAnna smiled and thanked the server for her help, then turned and walked quickly out of the diner. Once outside she tried to think of why her friend would miss work. She thought about what Lydia had said about Jacob, and how she thought he was coming back to her soon. Could that have happened last night?

JoAnna didn't want to think about that right now. All she wanted was to find Lydia and say goodbye, then get out of this horrible little town. She was sure she could remember the way to Lydia's trailer and once out on the road, she made a few turns and when she passed the Post Office she knew she was headed in the right direction. After a few minutes, she found the trailer. In the driveway sat Lydia's car.

JoAnna got out of her car and walked up to the trailer. She could see through the front windows into the kitchen but there was no movement inside. Surely Lydia had heard her drive up so why was she not coming to the door? When she looked down and noticed muddy footprints on the porch, she thought about Jacob.

"Lydia?" she said as she rapped on the small diamond-shaped window in the middle of the door. She rang the doorbell again, but no one answered. She walked over and looked through the kitchen window and saw dirty dishes in the sink, then looked over her shoulder at Lydia's car. This wasn't making any sense. Then she walked back to the door, tried the doorknob and was surprised to find it unlocked. She paused for a moment to gather her wits, then stepped into the trailer.

"Lydia? Are you here? It's me, JoAnna." There was no response. A frown crossed her face when she looked towards the kitchen and the hall that led to the bedroom. She hoped Lydia would appear in the hallway in her PJ's, wiping the sleep out of her eyes.

JoAnna saw her duffel bag on the couch and fought the urge to just grab it and be on her way. She didn't want to leave without saying goodbye but it was becoming apparent that maybe that was the best thing for her to do. Then she heard something stir in the bedroom at the end of the hall.

"Lydia?" JoAnna said as she walked through the kitchen to the hallway. She heard the sound again. Lydia was obviously sleeping late and skipping out on work.

When JoAnna reached the bedroom door she peaked around the doorframe and saw a man sleeping in Lydia's bed. She could tell by looking at the other side of the bed that someone had been in bed with him.

JoAnna gasped and backed away from the door. Then she turned and tried to move as quickly down the hallway as she could without making noise. She grabbed her bag off the couch, slung it over her shoulder and was about to turn towards the door when she heard another noise.

The man stepped into the hallway and started walking towards her. When he passed the small hall window, the morning sun illuminated his face and JoAnna immediately recognized him. She could see the dark, coal-like eyes.

"Stay away from me!" JoAnna turned and ran across the living room. When she got to the front door she tripped over the bottom of the doorframe and fell through the door onto the deck. She struggled to her feet and ran down the length of the deck to the stairs. Once back in her car, she threw her duffel bag onto the seat and tried to start the engine. But when she pushed the button on the dash, nothing happened. She pushed it several more times, cursing under her breath. Then she remembered the brake. When she put her foot on the pedal and pushed the button again, the engine roared to life.

JoAnna put the car in reverse, spinning the tires in the mud as she backed out of the driveway. It was time to leave, and whatever was going on in Lydia's trailer was not her concern. She wanted to see her friend before she left but that was obviously not meant to be. But it didn't matter now. All that mattered was getting to Charleston to find Paul.

21

JoAnna made her way back to Solomon's main street, then took the road out of town towards the Outer Banks. Rolling down the windows to let the cool air circulate though the car, she replayed the events of the past few days until her mind settled on her deal with Isabelle. Was it real? Had anything been real? She hoped so. Knowing she had just spent an entire year in a mental institution trying to cope with Paul's suicide, she hated to think that maybe she had turned into the kind of person that couldn't tell the difference between the real world and the world inside her head.

JoAnna had not spoken to her mother since yesterday. Where was she? Why was she not answering her phone? If something had happened to her why hadn't one of her mother's friends called her? She was sure they had her cell phone number. Why the silence? As JoAnna pondered this, she noticed an approaching road sign about the Pamlico Sound ferry. She turned down the road and it wasn't long before she found herself at the ferry landing. Several hundred yards from the landing she could see the ferry approaching on the hazy blue water.

She pulled up behind the two cars waiting at the landing and then got out and walked over to the small tackle shop near the pier. Behind the cash register of the walk-up window sat a girl with blonde hair and hazel-green eyes.

"I'd like a ticket to Ocracoke, please," JoAnna said.

"Will that be all, ma'am?" the girl said as she worked the cash register. JoAnna spied a small bobble head fisherman sitting on the counter and resisted the urge to buy it. She picked it up and watched its head wobble back and forth.

"Ma'am?"

"Oh, yes. I'm sorry. That'll be all." She sat the bobble head down on the counter and took the ticket, then turned and walked back to her car. Once inside she leaned back in the seat and tried to relax, hoping that once she had a body of water in between her and the town of Solomon it would help her straighten out the events of the past few days.

One of the deckhands started directing the cars onto the ferry but JoAnna didn't see him. She was busy watching a fisherman work his rod and reel at the end of the pier. When another deckhand patted her side window, it jolted her out of her reverie. She smiled sheepishly and started her car, then pulled onto the ferry.

After about ten minutes, she felt a nudge as the captain pulled away from the dock. Once clear of the landing the diesel engines rumbled to life, and the ferry started its route to Ocracoke Island. A flock of seagulls hovered over the bow, swooping down to the deck two or three at a time to retrieve potato chips thrown to them by one of the passengers. JoAnna watched the birds for a few minutes until the lulling motion of the ferry made her drowsy. Unable to fight the urge any longer, she reclined her seat and drifted into a nap.

The dream was vague. She could see Paul in their home in Charleston walking through the attic with his father's shotgun in his hand. Then the horrible sound of the shotgun blast jolted her awake. She sat up in the seat and it took a few moments for her to remember where she was at. As her breathing returned to normal, she looked out over the hazy expanse of the Pamlico Sound. Her earlier thoughts about being crazy and needing more therapy returned to her mind, but deep down inside she knew she was okay. She refused let herself believe that she was losing her mind, so she decided to stop thinking about it. There was nothing wrong with her. Solomon was real and so was Wicked Izzy.

You must journey to the place where he left this world, JoAnna... Isabelle's words drifted through her head.

"The place where he left this world..." JoAnna repeated the words to herself as she looked out across the Sound.

JoAnna knew this meant Charleston and the house where Paul had killed himself in the attic. If she was going to believe that Wicked Izzy was real, and that the deal she made with her was real, then she knew Charleston was where she had to go. The alternative was to drive back to Spartanburg and tell her mother the entire story about Solomon and then be readmitted to the Morgan Institute for another year's worth of therapy. No, she was not crazy and she would not be traveling back to Spartanburg for anything.

Thinking about this, she pulled her phone out of her purse and dialed her mother's number. She listened once again to the robotic voicemail before leaving another message. Where in the hell was her mother? The fact that her mother had made the complete flip from watching over her too closely and calling her incessantly, to not even returning her phone calls astounded her. It just didn't make any sense, she thought, frowning at her phone.

"Just what is the deal, Mom? Where are you?" she whispered as she dropped the phone back in her purse. She looked up at the sun overhead and realized that if she was really going to Charleston that she would probably have to spend the night somewhere along the way. She felt a shiver as she thought about arriving in Charleston after dark. There was no way she was going to go to her old house in the middle of the night. Only a crazy person would do such a thing.

Only a crazy person... JoAnna chuckled and shook her head. Not only did she find this amusing, she found the whole situation amusing. Here she was riding a ferry to an island she had never been to before and at the same time trying to coordinate her arrival in Charleston with the time of day she felt would be best suited for meeting her dead husband. "On second thought, maybe I really am crazy," she said as she looked out across the water at the approaching shoreline of the island.

The dock pilings drift by as the captain directed the ferry to the dock. The engines reversed and a soft bump followed as the ferry bow contacted the dock. JoAnna's car was the last one to leave the ferry and when she rolled past one of the deckhands, she stopped and rolled down her window.

"Excuse me, but when does the ferry leave for Cedar Island?"

"It's coming in right now," the deckhand said as he nodded towards the harbor entrance.

Once on the Cedar Island ferry, JoAnna thought about the remaining trip ahead of her. She figured that she would need to stop for the night about halfway to Charleston since there was no reason for her to be on the road late at night. She would try to find a nicer motel than the Swamp Fox Inn, then in the morning she would drive into Charleston and go to her old house. One way or another she knew that she was going to find out if Wicked Izzy's power was real. Either Paul would be at the house as promised, or he would not. More than likely, he would not be there and she would sit in the driveway of the house feeling like a complete fool.

She thought about seeing Jacob in Lydia's trailer, about Pike and Ray, then about the cemetery and the names on the tombstones. None of it really proved anything. Maybe at this very moment, Isabelle Pearl and Lydia, and the rest of them, were sitting in the diner having a good laugh about the fun they had just had with the girl from out of town. Maybe it was just a cruel joke. *No one returns from the dead…* she thought as she drifted off to sleep.

When the ferry nudged against the dock, JoAnna woke up and gathered herself. She disembarked and made her way down the highway to Morehead City, past Jacksonville until she was on Highway 17 south. An hour passed before she crested a bridge over a tidal basin and saw the approaching lights of Wilmington burning white beneath the blood red horizon. On the outskirts of town, she found a decent looking hotel and decided to stop for the night.

Once in her room she bolted the door and checked the closet and the bathroom just to make sure she was alone. She stretched out on the bed and turned on the TV, flipping past each channel until she found a rerun of one of her favorite movies. For the first time in a long while she finally felt safe. And she was also three floors up, having specified to the man at the registration desk that she didn't want a ground floor room. If she could just get hold of her mother, she would feel even better, but she had all but given up hope on that.

After watching her movie for a little while, she got up and took a hot shower figuring it would help her sleep better. After all, tomorrow was going to be a big day, she thought as the soothing hot water washed over her head and down her back. Tomorrow she would see Paul. JoAnna thought about this as she ran her hands through her hair before bringing them down to her cheeks.

"Listen to me… Tomorrow I see Paul… JoAnna Stedford you are as crazy as a loon," she said as she reached for the soap. "Maybe I can get my old room back when they check me into the Morgan Institute." She smiled at this as she rubbed the soap over her legs. But in the back of her mind, she still held firm to the idea that she was perfectly sane. In fact, she knew she was. But it just seemed easier to joke about it than to admit that she had little doubt in the power of Wicked Izzy to keep up her end of the bargain. Solomon was real, Wicked Izzy was real, and tomorrow she would see her husband again.

Once out of the shower, she dried her hair and slipped into her nightshirt. She crawled into the large king-sized bed and tried to find another movie on TV. But the only thing playing were news programs and a few reality shows. She clicked the power button on the remote and tossed it on the bed beside her, then pulled the covers up to her chin. Sleep came quickly.

22

JoAnna pulled off the road and stared out across the overgrown lawn at the house she and Paul had shared together. A broken window with a crooked shutter caught her eye as she scanned the front of the abandoned house. At the end of the gravel driveway, now pockmarked with patches of weeds, she spied the old mailbox post Paul had planted just after they moved in.

Gathering her strength, she walked over to the post and found the mailbox lying next to it in the tall weeds, the name STEDFORD displayed in stick-on letters across the side. She remembered the day they took a selfie of themselves standing next to the mailbox, their first home in the background.

Her eyes followed the driveway again until they settled on the point where it ended under the live oak next to the house. Beyond the oak sat the small gardening shed in the backyard, its door askew on the hinges. It reminded her of the shed at Paul's house in Bellville.

JoAnna took a few steps up the driveway and stopped, unable to walk any further. Images of the life she and Paul had shared in the house during their first year together rushed through her mind. Just as she felt herself slipping deeper into her reverie, a crow cawed from behind her. She turned and saw the bird sitting on the mailbox post as it studied her with its dark eyes.

The desire to see Paul was the only source of courage she had, and this helped her take one more step up the driveway. As soon as she moved, the crow cawed again from the post. When she turned and looked at the bird, it took flight and flew across the yard to the roof of the house.

Filling her lungs with air, she took another step towards the house. Paul was here, she knew it, but she didn't know where to find him. Maybe he was inside waiting on her, perhaps even watching her from a window. Her eyes scanned the house again but the only movement came from the crow walking along the peak of the roof.

"Paul?" JoAnna called out across the yard. She waited and when there was no response, she called out again. Only the crow responded. The resounding caw echoed through the air and out across the marsh that bordered the far edge of the backyard. Just when she was about to give up hope, she noticed movement in the side door. Panic flashed through her body as she watched the side door open. It took every ounce of courage she could muster to stand her ground and not turn and run down the driveway back to her car.

When Paul saw her through the window in the door, recognition bloomed on his face. JoAnna stood motionless, her heart hammering in her chest as he made his way down the steps. Once at the bottom he smiled at her and held out his arms. Wearing his favorite pair of jeans with a white T-shirt, his arm looked so inviting that it was all JoAnna could do not to run to him. This is what she had been waiting for, but she couldn't shake the feeling that something was wrong.

"Jo…" Paul said as he held out his arms. Her eyes swelled with tears at the sound of his voice. "Come to me." Her chin quivered, and she brought her hand up to cover her mouth. Tears streamed down her face as she looked at Paul standing less than ten feet away from her.

"Sweet JoAnna, I've waiting so long to see you. Come to me."

JoAnna dropped her hands and rushed forward. When their bodies met, Paul wrapped his arms around her and held her tightly. She buried her face in his neck and took in a long breath, relishing his familiar scent. Love rushed through her chest and for a moment she felt as if she would pass out.

"It's okay, baby. I've got you."

JoAnna squeezed Paul with her face still buried in his neck. Then she moved her face to the smooth cotton of his T-shirt and smelled the scent of laundry detergent. It really was him. Wicked Izzy had made good on her promise.

They held each other for a few moments, neither saying a word. When they parted, JoAnna looked into Paul's face and placed her hands on his cheeks. They felt warm and inviting. *What Wicked Izzy brings back can be touched, felt, loved…* Lydia's words drifted through her mind when she felt Paul's warm skin under her hands. When their lips met, the entire world fell away. It was as if they had never been apart. Every nerve ending in her body fired, sending electric chills all the way down her legs.

"It's okay, Jo. Everything is okay," Paul said. JoAnna looked into his eyes and then hugged him again, this time even tighter. She closed her eyes and put her face on his shoulder again but this time the feeling was different. In place of soft cotton, she felt the course material of a formal suit coat.

JoAnna opened her eyes and when she saw the dark blue material instead of the white cotton T-shirt, she pushed Paul away. A scream crawled up her throat. Instead of jeans and a T-shirt, he wore his dark blue burial suit. Mortuary thread stitched across his neck and up the side of his face where the mortician had attempted to sew his face back together from the shotgun blast.

"Come to me," Paul said, his voice hoarse and strained.

JoAnna gasped and sat bolt upright up in the bed, breathing hard as adrenalin thundered through her veins. Disoriented, it took her a few seconds to realize she was in a motel room. Then she remembered stopping for the night on her way to Charleston. She covered her face with her hands and just as she felt herself beginning to calm down, she looked over at the window and saw the outline of a person silhouetted against the silvery drapes. She reached for the lamp but when she turned it on, no one was there.

Still disoriented, JoAnna got out of bed and checked the door. The privacy latch was still in place along with the deadbolt. She checked the bathroom and then stepped back to the foot of the bed. No one was in the room. She went to the bathroom, leaned against the sink, and tried to collect herself. She looked down into the sink and closed her eyes for a few moments, and when she raised her eyes again, she saw her mother standing behind her, a worried look on her face.

"JoAnna, no…" her mother whispered as their eyes met in the reflection. But when she turned around, her mother was gone.

JoAnna slid down the front of the sink cabinet and sat down on the floor. She wrapped her arms around her knees as terror and confusion overtook her. After she finished crying, she gathered herself together and returned to bed. She left the bathroom light on and turned on the TV once she was under the covers. Thoughts of what awaited her in Charleston tumbled through her mind, tempered with the nightmare of Paul in his funeral suit and the image of her mother warning her about something. After an hour of tossing and turning, she fell into a dreamless sleep until her alarm clock buzzed her awake at 6 am.

23

JoAnna stopped on the way to Charleston and got a biscuit in a drive thru and two hours later found herself at the entrance to Palmview Cemetery, less than a mile down the road from her and Paul's old house. She wasn't ready to see the house yet, especially after the horrible dream from the night before, so she had decided to visit the cemetery first.

As she drove into the cemetery her thoughts darkened. It contained the grave of her only child, a child she had never even had a chance to hold, and beside that was Paul's grave. It would be the first time she had seen either grave since Paul's funeral. She thought about this as she rolled slowly along the winding road.

Paul's grave was unimportant now, she reasoned. Lydia had told her that the person Wicked Izzy brought back was not some sort of rotten corpse that rose up out of the ground, so what was inside of Paul's coffin was not what she would see when the time came. But deep down inside, the whole idea still felt ridiculous.

She got out of the car and walked through several rows of tombstones until she was standing next to Justin's grave. After wiping away grass cuttings on the footstone, she read the name engraved in the granite. *Justin William Stedford...* Tears rolled down her cheeks as she read the birth and death dates. They were the same. Her eyes turned to the larger granite tombstone beside Justin's.

"Oh Paul... I miss you so much." She paused for a moment while the words gathered in her throat. "Please come back to me."

JoAnna looked around her to see if anyone else was in the cemetery, then got down on her knees between the two graves. "She said I would see you if I came back to the place where you left me..."

she whispered. "I will be there today. Please come back to me. *Please…*" She stood up and took few steps backwards thinking there was no need for all this sadness. Soon Izzy would make good on her end of the bargain, and after that she would be happy again.

A cool wind rushed through the cemetery, bringing with it the smell rain. JoAnna looked up at the dark clouds and then turned to walk towards her car. Just as she closed the door, the sky opened in a torrential downpour so heavy that it made her feel claustrophobic. She looked out of the windshield and over her shoulder to the rear of the car but the only thing she could make out was the fuzzy outline of the large oak tree standing close by.

She put her face close to the glass of the driver's side window and squinted to see through the pouring rain. Her eyes widened when she saw what looked like a person standing in the pouring rain between the rows of tombstones. She leaned closer to the window again and tried to focus on the shape. When she saw that it was moving towards her, she felt her spirits rise.

"Paul!"

JoAnna watched the figure move towards her. Who else could it be? Even though she wasn't at the house, maybe the cemetery was close enough to satisfy Wicked Izzy's instructions about returning to the place where his soul left the world. The toxic mix of fear and hope made her feel lightheaded. Paul was here, but she didn't know what to do. Should she jump out and run to his arms in the pouring rain? Just the thought of such a thing filled her with joy. Wicked Izzy had made good on her promise, and the proof was walking towards her through the rain.

"Paul…" JoAnna whispered as she put her hand on the door handle. Just as she was about to open the door and run to Paul, she felt a pang of doubt. When her eyes focused again on the figure, she realized that it wasn't Paul. She watched in horror as her mother stepped up to the window of the car.

JoAnna screamed and tried to push herself away from the window when she saw her mother's dark, piercing eyes staring at her through the glass. When she finally got the engine started, she stepped down hard on the gas pedal causing the rear end of the car to fishtail in the wet grass. Once she made it onto the pavement, the tires grabbed hold and propelled her forward at a speed too fast for her to handle. She skidded through a sharp curve and then down an embankment, throwing her arms up in front of her face just as the car slammed into a large pine tree. The resulting impact deployed the airbag and knocked her unconscious.

24

JoAnna was unsure of how long she had been unconscious when her eyes finally flickered open. She looked around and then gasped at the sight of the deflated air bag. Through the windshield, she saw the front end of the car crushed against the tree and knew that it was undrivable. The rain was still coming down hard and darkness was fast approaching. She knew she had to get out of the car and the cemetery and make her way to the house before it was too late.

Relieved that she was unharmed, JoAnna collected herself and looked around the interior of the car. She didn't care about anything other than getting out and up the embankment to the road. She pulled hard on the door handle and after a brief struggle was able to get the door open. When her feet hit the mud beneath the door, she slipped and fell onto her back.

Cursing under her breath, she got to her feet and clambered up the muddy embankment. Once at the top she looked back out over the cemetery towards the graves, knowing she would never return to them again. Her life was in the other direction, waiting for her in her old house. Once she got to the house and felt Paul's arms around her, her new life would begin.

As she made her way to the entrance of the cemetery, JoAnna thought about her mother. It was obvious to her now that her mother had come to a bad end, probably due to the handiwork of Isabelle Pearl. With her mother gone she realized that she was alone, and even though Isabelle had told her being alone was not a condition of her help, JoAnna now knew better. Isabelle had lied to her, probably knowing at that very moment that her mother was already dead. JoAnna forced this out of her mind. Her mother was gone, but if it was a condition of having Paul back, then so be it. He was her everything, and she had come too far to give up on him now.

The rain was falling even harder as JoAnna left the cemetery and struck out along the road towards her old house. Shaking from the cold, she pushed through the sheets of rain as she made her way up the side of the highway. Paul's warm embrace awaited her and he would make everything all right if she could just make it to the house.

Thick woods, dark and foreboding, lined both sides of the road. The trees swayed in unison in the face of the wind as JoAnna continued on through the rain. When the voice came, it blended with the sound of the wind rushing through the trees.

JoAnna... Nooooo...

"Leave me alone, Mother! I love him!" she shouted through the rain at ghostly apparition standing in the middle of the road. "I love him!" Anger flashed through her body as she spun around and resumed her pace along the edge of the highway. After a few steps, she looked over her shoulder and saw that her mother's ghost was gone.

When she came to a small bridge crossing over a creek, JoAnna stopped and leaned against the railing to catch her breath. She looked down at the water rushing under the bridge and heard her mother's voice again.

Noooo...

The cold rain and wind only tightened her resolve to get to the house. She knew Paul would make everything better once she found him. His embrace would comfort her and warm her down to the depths of her soul. All she had to do was get to the house. That was where he left the world, and that was where he would return to her just as Izzy had promised.

A sudden gust of wind knocked her off balance and nearly caused her to fall over the bridge railing. But she caught the edge and steadied herself. Shivering from the cold, with nightfall fast approaching, she wanted to get to the house as soon as she could. The thought of entering her old house in the dark terrified her, but if it came to that she knew she would just have to find the courage to do it.

In her rush to get to the house to see Paul, JoAnna had not given much thought to what she would do if someone was living in the house. She remembered what her mother told her about the bank repossession, and how someone else probably owned the house now. She felt her spirits fall. How would all this work if someone was living in the house? The only hope she had was that the house would be standing empty.

As JoAnna made it up the incline, the road turned to the left. She knew that the house was just beyond the curve. The storm intensified and a loud crack of thunder startled her, causing her to step off the road onto the median. She stumbled and fell, then slid down the muddy embankment to the edge of the swollen creek.

"You're not going to stop me!" she yelled into the surrounding trees. She rolled over in the mud and got up onto her hands and knees, then clambered up the embankment until she was back on the road. Wiping the mud from her face, she got to her feet and regained her bearings. Something was trying to stop her from getting to the house, but she refused to surrender to it.

When JoAnna saw the house, she quickened her pace until she was standing across the street from the driveway. She realized the mail box had not suffered the same fate as the one in her nightmare and felt a glimmer of hope when she read the word STEDFORD on the side. The windows of the house were dark, and no cars were parked in the driveway. To her relief, the house looked vacant.

Soaked down to her bones from the pouring rain, she felt a shiver run through her body as she walked up the driveway. Her hands were shaking and her breathing was short and shallow and as she got closer to the house, she could see that it had fallen into disrepair. Someone had broken out a window, and the grass in the yard was tall and full of weeds. When she got closer to the house, she stopped and stared at the front door, then heard the wind rush through the trees, along with the voice of her mother.

Stay away from him, JoAnna...

When she heard her mother's warning, JoAnna knew she was at a crossroads, and if she entered the house her life would change forever. Could she just turn around and run away? Was it that simple? She had made a deal with Wicked Izzy, and she had no doubt that if she entered the house that Izzy would make good on that deal. But what if she didn't enter the house? What if she just turned around right now and left? She could run down the driveway and flag down the first passing car and beg them for help. Would that free her from the deal she had made with Izzy? If she never actually saw Paul, never touched him, or felt his embrace, would she still owe Wicked Izzy for her services? If she ran away now, could she live the rest of her life free of any obligation to their deal? JoAnna looked around her at the overgrown yard of her old house as the wind whispered through the trees again.

JoAnna... Nooooo...

As the rain pelted her face and danced on the ground around her feet, JoAnna Stedford looked at the house again and made her final decision.

A deal is a deal, she whispered as she looked up at the dark windows.

25

JoAnna stopped at the end of the gravel driveway and looked in the backyard at the shed sitting in the rain, its one lone window long since broken out. It reminded her of Bellville. But there was no need to go to the shed to look for Paul. Izzy had said that he would return to the place where his soul left the world, and that place was the attic.

As she walked towards the house, she thought about the journey that had led her to this point. The year of therapy after Paul's suicide and how they had told her she was crazy, her trip to Solomon, meeting Lydia and then her night at Izzy's house. She thought about the deal they made. The requirement that a person be alone in the world to receive Izzy's help now made perfect sense to her. When she walked out of the house tonight with Paul, there would be no need to explain him to anyone. They could start a new life together and no one would ever have to know about their past.

JoAnna shivered in the cold rain as she climbed the steps to the porch. When she looked through the screen, it brought back memories of having morning coffee with Paul while contemplating the day's yardwork ahead of them. A year ago, this memory would have saddened her but those days were over with now. Paul was waiting for her in the attic, and many mornings together were ahead of them.

The wind roared through the trees when JoAnna stepped onto the porch. When she heard the familiar voice warning her away again, she turned and looked through the screen towards the dark woods lining the backyard.

"I love him, Mother!" she yelled towards the tree line.

Finding the back door to the house locked, JoAnna returned to the bottom of the steps and picked up a small landscaping brick from the edge of the flowerbed. She threw it through the window of the backdoor and listened as it landed and rolled across the kitchen floor. Once she got the door open, she peered into the dark kitchen and felt another cold shiver rush down her back. Her mother's voice, carrying with it her final warning, whispered again from the trees. JoAnna realized that once she crossed the threshold, there would be no turning back. With her heart hammering in her chest, she took one last look at the woods behind her and then stepped into the kitchen.

Nothing happened when she flicked the light switch by the door, so she felt her way along the counter until she found their old junk drawer, hoping that it still held their stash of candles and matches. Once she found a candle and got it lit, she held it out in front of her and surveyed her surroundings. The flickering light from the candle cast crooked shadows around her but only made her feel even more isolated inside the cavernous house. Summoning all the courage she could, she crept through the kitchen and into the living room and when she tiptoed around the sofa, she heard a dull *thump* upstairs. She jerked around so quickly that her movement almost extinguished the candle.

"Paul?" Her voice echoed through the empty house as the windows flashed silver from a bolt of lightning. Then she called out again.

"Paul? It's me, JoAnna."

Goosebumps rose on the back of her neck as she walked towards the foot of the stairs, but when her foot caught the edge of a throw rug, she tripped and fell. The candle winked out and rolled away in the darkness and after frantically patting the floor around her, she finally found it and got it relit using the book of matches in her pocket. As the flame grew on the end of the candle, she cursed at the throw rug and then turned her attention to the dark staircase in front of her.

Standing alone at the foot of the stairs with only her candle to hold back the darkness, JoAnna knew she was teetering on the edge of insanity. Her mother was gone, and she was alone. No one was looking for her. No one even knew where she was at. Then she felt her resolve strengthen. Yes, she was alone, but that was about to change. The love of her life was waiting for her upstairs, and he would put an end to her loneliness forever.

One step at a time, she climbed the stairs until her head was level with the second floor. She stopped and raised the candle so that it illuminated the hallway, then took a few more steps until she was standing at the top of the stairs.

The bedroom doors cast oblong shadows as she moved down the hallway. When she reached the master bedroom, she stepped into the doorway and extended her arm to illuminate the room. Several of the dresser drawers were open, with pieces of clothing hanging over the edges. The sheets and blanket were gone from the bed.

Suddenly a sharp bolt of lightning lit the windows, followed by a crack of thunder. JoAnna jumped but managed to hold on to the candle. She moved away from the master bedroom and to the door of Justin's nursery. When she raised the candle and looked into the room, a rush of sorrow engulfed her. But there was no time to dwell on this. Paul waited for her in the attic and she wanted to get to him as soon as possible. She took one more look at the nursery and closed the door, then turned her attention to the attic door above her and the pullcord dangling beneath it.

She reached up and touched the plastic knob on the end of the cord but made no effort to pull on it to extend the stairs. Once again, the idea of stopping all this by running out of the house rushed through her mind. She could still leave and put an end to this madness, but she knew she would never find another man like Paul. She thought about how far she had come to get to this point, and how the only thing separating her from the love of her life now was the wooden trapdoor to the attic. JoAnna released the plastic knob and let her hand fall to her side. She stared into the flame on the candle, closed her eyes and gathered her strength.

When her eyes opened, they were dark and full of carnal desire. Paul awaited her in the attic and she needed to feel his arms around her. She pulled on the cord and worked the stairs until she managed to get them unfolded, then stared up at the black rectangle above her.

Pausing every few steps to collect herself, JoAnna climbed the ladder being careful with the candle in her hand. Once at the top, she lifted her arm and scanned the circle of light thrown off by the candle, then felt her heart sink in her chest.

The attic was empty.

She exhaled a long breath of disappointment, climbed the rest of the way up the ladder and stepped off onto the plywood floor. The candle in her hand lit the small area around her but the far corners of the attic remained shrouded in darkness. All she could see was the water heater and a few boxes of assorted junk. Next to the boxes sat a stack of old newspapers she and Paul had saved to use when painting the inside of the house. She walked over to them while trying to ward off the feelings of foolishness creeping into her head. How could she have believed any of this? No one returns from the dead. Standing alone in the attic, JoAnna knew right then that she was crazy to ever have believed in any of this.

"JoAnna…"

The voice was soft and she couldn't tell if it had been real or just her imagination. Perhaps it was just the wind rushing through the eaves of the house. Then she heard it again, this time a bit louder.

"JoAnna…"

JoAnna froze, unable to turn towards the source of the voice. Her bottom lip quivered and tears stung the corners of her eyes, then she remembered Lydia's words.

What Wicked Izzy brings back can be touched, felt, loved…

JoAnna tightened her grasp on the candle and turned her body around to face whoever, or *whatever* was behind her. At first, she didn't see anything, but after a few seconds she watched as Paul stepped out of the darkness and into the dim circle of candlelight.

Dressed in an old pair of faded jeans and a T-shirt, he looked completely normal. She remembered the night she found him in the attic just over a year ago, a large chunk of his face missing from the shotgun blast. Now his face was perfect again and covered with the grin that she had fell in love with on the day she first met him.

JoAnna stared at Paul and knew that at any minute she would wake up from this dream and find herself alone in a motel room soaking wet from the night sweats. This could not be real. There was no way her dead husband was standing in front of her looking just as youthful and unharmed as he did on their wedding day.

"Paul…" JoAnna croaked into the darkness, fighting back the tears. The candle wobbled in her hand causing the shadows to dance around them. Paul studied her as he stood motionless in the dim light.

"Sweet JoAnna… I've missed you so much," he said as he raised his arms.

When Paul took a step towards her, it was more than she could take. Fear scalded every nerve ending in her body and out reflex she took a step backwards. Contact with her dead husband, or whatever he was, just didn't seem possible. What she was seeing had to be a ghost.

What Wicked Izzy brings back can be touched, felt, loved...

Touched... Could she really touch him? But JoAnna couldn't bring herself to reach out to the apparition standing in front of her. Instead she took another step backwards until she felt the cold steel of the water heater against her back. Paul only smiled. He understood her fear but also knew it was pointless.

"Don't be afraid, Jo. It's me."

Instead of reaching out, JoAnna pushed against the water heater and held the candle in front of her for protection. She was afraid of what she would feel if she touched him. Would his hands be cold and clammy, or would they be as warm as hers?

Paul smiled again. "Don't be afraid."

JoAnna, noooo.... The voice of her mother circulated around her in the still air of the attic. JoAnna turned her head and looked in the direction of the attic stairs and then back at Paul. He seemed to be unaware of the sound of her mother's voice.

"Please, Jo. Let me hold you," Paul said, his eyes pleading with her.

Suddenly something inside of her snapped, and she felt the strength return to her legs. What was standing in front of her was what she had asked for. Wicked Izzy had made good on her side of their deal and now Paul was right in front of her with his hand extended, asking her to come to him. This was her second chance to be with him. The touch she had been craving for over a year was now only moments away. She stiffened against the water heater, then took one step forward. Then she heard the soft whisper of her mother's voice once again.

Don't touch him, JoAnna...

JoAnna ignored the warning. She reached out for Paul's hand and when he wrapped his fingers around hers, they felt warm and comforting. He was not cold like a corpse. Relief flushed through her body when she realized that Lydia had told her the truth. Her body quivered, and she felt light-headed when she looked into Paul's eyes illuminated by the yellow light of the candle. The touch of his hand was wonderful, and she never wanted to let go. Then he took a step forward and raised his other arm. The warm embrace she had dreamed of for so long was about to happen. She felt her entire body tingle in anticipation.

Paul moved close to her and put his arms around her. She put her face in the crook of his neck and closed her eyes as his arms tightened around her. It had been so long since she had felt his touch and it felt more wonderful than ever. She breathed in his scent as she slid her arm around his body. In the other hand she held the candle, its yellow light fighting to hold back the surrounding darkness.

When JoAnna lifted her face and looked into Paul's eyes she noticed they had changed. They now seemed full of sadness. He placed his hands on her cheeks and she felt dizzy from the pleasure of his touch. Then he spoke to her in a soft whisper.

"JoAnna... What have you done?"

Outside the storm raged. There were no windows in the attic but JoAnna could see the flashes of lightning through the vent on the far side of the attic wall. The thunder boomed, assaulting the house from all directions.

"What have you done?" Paul asked again. She felt his embrace loosen. A loud clap of thunder sounded outside, followed by another low rumble. She was not sure how to answer him. He released her and took a step backwards, leaving her to stand on her own.

"I... I wanted you back, Paul. I can't live without you. You left me too early. We had our whole life to spend together. She said I could have you back. Her name is..."

"I know who she is, JoAnna. We all know who she is. She put us where we are. Why did you go to her?"

"Because I love you, Paul... That's all you need to know. We can be together now. Everyone that knew us before you died is gone. It's just you and me now." Paul's face saddened and sympathy pooled in his eyes.

"Oh JoAnna..." he finally said as he stepped closer to her again. He placed a hand on her cheek and once again the warmth of his touch made her head swim with delight. When she looked into his eyes, her heart fluttered in her chest and a wave of dizziness hit her. A few seconds later, she fainted and fell to the attic floor. Paul watched the candle as it landed beside her, its flame flickering as it hit the floor. It rolled and came to rest against the stack of old newspapers, setting the on fire almost immediately. Within seconds, the fire spread from the newspapers to the nearby rafters.

Paul knew how important JoAnna was, and that he could not allow any harm to come to her. She was special, not only to him but to Isabelle Pearl. She could not fulfill her end of the bargain if she died in the fire, and he knew her soul would pay a horrible price if she could not settle with Isabelle Pearl when the time came. He lifted JoAnna over his shoulder and carried her down the attic stairs and out of the house. Once outside, he looked up and saw that the entire roof was on fire. Before long, the home they had once shared together would be gone forever.

26

The car hummed beneath them as Paul and JoAnna traveled down the dark, two-lane highway. There were no other cars around, nor were there any other signs of civilization. The trees lining the road rose out of the swamp water and formed a canopy over the highway, filtering out the moonlight. Paul held the wheel steady as the car sped along the road. JoAnna lay at his side, still unconscious from the ordeal she had suffered at the house.

Before long the trees receded and the canopy of branches disappeared, and the landscape opened to reveal rolling hills dotted with occasional stands of trees. Paul looked over at JoAnna and placed his hand on her thigh. "Jo..." he whispered as he gave her thigh a gentle shake. "JoAnna..." he said again, this time just a little louder.

When her eyes fluttered open, JoAnna sat up and looked out of the window at the passing scenery. Recognition bloomed on her face when she looked back at him.

"Paul!" she said. "What are we...? Where are...?" She looked around the interior of the car and frowned. "How did we get here?"

"Easy, Jo. Just calm down, everything is okay."

JoAnna adjusted her seat upright, then realized what car they were riding in.

"This is your old car. How did we...?"

"She thought it would make it easy for you."

"She?"

Paul shrugged his shoulders. "She thought you would like it. My old car, I mean."

As JoAnna settled back into her seat, Paul turned his head and stared through the front windshield. After a few moments he looked over at her sitting sheepishly in the passenger's seat, studying him as if she still couldn't accept that he was real. She let out a sigh of relief when her fingers touched his face. It was warm and soft. She withdrew her hand and covered her mouth, then squeezed his arm.

"You *are* real," she whispered. "She really did it. I thought what happened in the attic was just a dream, but you're really here."

Paul looked at her. "Yep, she really did it." He winked and patted the dash. "And she even gave us back my old beater."

JoAnna shifted in her seat and let her eyes scan the dashboard of Paul's old car from college. She recognized everything about it right down to the small star in the windshield caused by a pebble on their honeymoon trip.

"Can I… Can I ask where we're going?" she said.

Paul didn't reply. After a few seconds he pointed through the windshield at a large billboard floating in the darkness off to the right, just above the trees.

"Summerland," she said as she read the single word painted in huge red letters across the top of the billboard. Underneath the word was the image of a Ferris wheel. The rest of the billboard carried a scene from a boardwalk.

"Summerland?" JoAnna repeated as the billboard glided past the car. "What is that? Or, *where* is that?"

Paul didn't want to tell her the truth so he just said, "Let's find out together."

"Summerland…" JoAnna whispered the word again and couldn't quite put a finger on where she had heard it before.

"Seems I've heard of that but I can't remember where." Then she resigned herself to the idea that she was riding through the countryside in her dead husband's old car with him at the wheel. She had to be insane. Soon she would wake up and find herself eating red Jell-O in her room at the Morgan Institute and telling the nurse all about her crazy dream.

The road looked completely unfamiliar to her. Paul remained silent behind the wheel but he cast a glance her way every few minutes to check on her. Finally, she worked up the courage to speak.

"I've missed you. Nothing was the same without you."

He turned and smiled. "I've missed you too. I missed you so

much that sometimes I would come to you at night just to watch you sleep. I would touch your face and wish I could be with you."

"Why did you... I mean, in the attic like that?" JoAnna said after a long pause.

"I had no choice, Jo. My soul was just a bargaining chip to that woman."

JoAnna's spine tingled. She was right about Nancy Stedford and the price she had paid Wicked Izzy. No life beyond her own...

"I'm not mad at you for what you did, but all that's in the past now."

When Paul reached over and took JoAnna's hand, she felt her heart swell inside her chest. She didn't know if any of this was real, or if she was insane, but whatever world she had stepped into, or Paul had stepped out of, was fine with her at the moment. The feel of Paul's hand was worth whatever it had taken to get her to this point.

JoAnna thought about this as she looked out the window at the dark countryside. The *past*... At this point she wasn't sure about what that meant. The past, the present, the future... She wasn't even sure what dimension she was in. She looked over at Paul and decided that wherever she was, whatever time and place, was fine with her. She could feel his hand in hers and she knew that was enough, and she didn't care that one day she would pay a price for it. That wasn't happening right now. Right now, she held Paul's hand in her own. What tomorrow would bring, if there was a tomorrow, didn't matter.

JoAnna resigned herself to her fate and squeezed Paul's hand again. Then she saw another billboard ahead, its bright light spilling down onto the side of the hill. It depicted a scene from the Old West. Across the top of the billboard was the word *Summerland* painted in bright yellow letters, followed by *Visit Our Authentic Saloon.*

When the billboard passed, JoAnna felt the car slow down. When Paul took the exit and came to a stop, she looked around and noticed there were no signs of life anywhere. No gas stations, restaurants or other cars.

"Where are we going?" she said as Paul turned right at the stop sign.

"We're almost there," he said.

The canopy of trees overhead returned, blotting out the moonlight. They traveled down the highway for a few minutes before Paul brought the car to a stop in the middle of the road. Standing in the glow of the headlights sat a crooked signpost with an arrow pointing to a narrow road leading into the woods. On the sign was the hand painted word *Summerland.*

"We're here, Jo. This is her place."

27

When Paul turned and started down the narrow road, JoAnna saw another billboard approaching. This one carried the image of a large, colorfully lit building and the words *Shag in the Pavilion!* After a few minutes, another billboard displaying a large, wooden a roller coaster drifted by.

"We must be going to the county fair," JoAnna said, hoping Paul would laugh.

"Yep," Paul said. "The fair... Or something like that."

After a few minutes, a pastel glow appeared just above the treetops ahead of them. When they rounded the curve, they saw a Ferris wheel off to their left, its lights ablaze against the night sky. JoAnna recognized it from one of the billboards.

Paul stopped the car next to the small ticket booth sitting in the middle of the road. An orange and white striped arm blocked the road. JoAnna looked over at the empty ticket booth and then at Paul, who was staring at the arm waiting for it to rise.

"No one is in the booth. What do we do now?"

"Just give it a second," Paul said. He turned his head and nodded at the booth as if he could see someone in it and when he did, the arm lifted. They pulled forward and continued down the road and when the tree line on their left ended, they were met with a colorful explosion of brilliant neon light. JoAnna was awestruck at the sight, but it didn't seem to faze Paul. He all but ignored the lights as he turned into the empty dirt parking lot and brought the car to a stop.

"We walk from here, Jo. Are you ready?"

Amazement blossomed on JoAnna's face as she looked at the amusement park in front of them. Signs advertising cotton candy, boardwalk fries and funnel cakes were everywhere. She tried to speak but couldn't find any words.

They got out of the car and Paul held JoAnna's hand as they walked through the gates into the park. Festive organ music filled the air, mixed with the clattering sound of the rides. Just ahead of them the Ferris wheel turned, it's multi-colored lights contrasting against the night sky. Off to the left sat the Pavilion. Skee Ball machines lined the back wall of the open first floor, and JoAnna watched as the softball-sized Skee balls, thrown by unseen hands, rolled down the small lanes and up into the rings centered on the backboards.

The rest of the Pavilion's bottom floor was empty. JoAnna noticed Paul staring at the Pavilion while the bells and lights of the Skee Ball machines rang out against the din of the surrounding rides. He shook his head and tugged at JoAnna's hand. "Come on, Jo. Let's walk."

Just past the Ferris wheel JoAnna saw the outline of a roller coaster ahead of them, its frame ablaze with long tubes of light. She could hear the clanking of the cars as they climbed the steep incline on their way to the top of the first drop. When she saw the bumper cars, she asked the question that had been bothering her since they stepped into the park. She turned and looked at Paul, squeezing his hand to get his attention. He knew what she was about to say.

"Paul, where are the people? I see bumper cars over there but no one is driving them. They're moving all by themselves. And look over there," she said, nodding in the direction of the Ferris wheel. "The baskets are empty."

JoAnna pointed at the row of games off to their right. She could see the water pistol game, its row of pistols shooting water into the mouths of clown heads lining the back wall of the booth. Each clown head had a balloon growing out of the top of it. Suddenly one of the balloons popped, and a bell went off.

"I'll explain later, Jo. Right now, we need to get moving."

As they turned and walked along the Midway, Paul remained silent while JoAnna marveled at her surroundings. This amusement park seemed to have every ride she had ever seen as a kid and in another time and place would have caused her to squeal with delight. But now she felt like she was walking through some sort of alien world where all the people had vanished.

As they continued along the Midway JoAnna looked into each

booth, expecting at any time to see a ghoulish Carnie staring back at her. But every booth was empty. When they came to an intersection in the Midway, she looked to her right and saw a huge funhouse sitting at the end of the row of game booths, the entrance marked by the open mouth of a large clown head. Colorful letters, each tilted at different angles, hung over the head.

The organ music grew louder as they moved down the Midway. When they stepped out of the row of game booths, they found the source of the music. JoAnna's mouth dropped open when she saw the pipe organ sitting in the center of the large, ornate Merry-Go-Round. Thousands of light bulbs adorned the ride, each blinking in time with the music to create a hypnotic light show. The well-detailed horses, each frozen in different stages of galloping, rose and fell as the ride turned, but were just as empty as the baskets on the Ferris wheel. Paul forced a smile when JoAnna noticed this and looked at him. He knew why she couldn't see the riders.

Suddenly huge clusters of fireworks lit up the sky. Surprised, JoAnna tilted her head back and watched the colorful display bloom above them.

"It's like this every night," Paul said in a wistful voice as he looked at fireworks and then at JoAnna. She was so innocent and beautiful, he thought to himself as he watched her take in the fireworks show. How could he have ever left her? And how could she have ended up here?

"Come on, Jo." Paul knew they needed to make it to the other side of the park so they could find a place for the night. He knew what would happen when dawn arrived and he wanted to get JoAnna somewhere safe.

Ahead to their right was a small trailer, its insides lit with bright yellow lights. Rows of candy apples sat across the counter on the front of the trailer. Above the candy apples hung spools of cotton candy. Across from the trailer, a small booth advertised pizza by the slice, and behind it she could see a miniature golf course. A windmill turned on one of the holes and next to it on an adjacent hole sat a large pirate's head. The sight of the miniature golf course brought back memories of the nights she had played at the beach with her father when she was a little girl.

When the Midway ended, Paul and JoAnna found themselves standing on a boardwalk that bordered the edge of a dark body of water. JoAnna thought about how many times she had stood on the boardwalk during summer vacations at the beach with her family. She had always been able to see blinking lights from boats off on the horizon. But this body of water was different. There were no lights in the distance, nothing to signal the presence of any sort of life beyond the shore. She looked out across the dark water and saw small waves lapping at the shoreline, their thin crests illuminated by the pastel glow of the park lights.

Beyond the amusement park sat an old wooden water tower lit from below by floodlights. Painted across the water tower was the word *Summerland*.

"The town," Paul said.

JoAnna frowned and said, "Have you been here before?"

At first Paul didn't answer. He only stared at the water tower in the distance. When he looked down at JoAnna, she could see the fear in his eyes.

"I've been here before," Paul said. "I was here when Isabelle brought me back to you. That's why I can see the people in the park and you can't. She pulled my soul out of Summerland and returned me to you and that's why you can't see anyone else. But the souls are all around us. Trust me, they're everywhere. Summerland is where they wait for Izzy to call them to their second life."

JoAnna's eyes widened, and she felt a shiver run down her body. She was more than ready to wake up from this nightmare. Paul sensed this and realized that he had probably told her more than she was ready to hear. He decided the best thing to do now was to just keep moving.

"Come on, Jo. The town isn't much but we can find a place for the night. I need to get you somewhere safe." He led her along the boardwalk while she stared out into the ghostly black ocean beyond the waves.

The miniature golf course spread to their left. JoAnna looked out across the small putting greens and tried to imagine people playing on it in the glare of the surrounding lights. She could still hear the organ music from the Merry-Go-Round and see the Ferris wheel over her shoulder, but as they moved farther down the boardwalk, the organ music started to fade.

Paul took JoAnna by the hand and guided her through an alleyway between two of the buildings. They emerged on the other side onto a narrow street lit by old-fashioned gas lamps perched on top of slender, wrought-iron poles. Dim flames flickered inside the lamps.

The cobblestone street reminded JoAnna of some of the old streets she and Paul had explored in Charleston right after they first moved to the town. The buildings lining the streets were small houses intermingled with storefronts, each with metal accordion-style gates pulled across the entrances. There were no signs of life anywhere. As they walked down the street through the yellow pools of gas light, the warm wind lifted JoAnna's hair off her shoulders.

"The wind is starting. We need to get inside," Paul said as he squeezed JoAnna's hand. His pace quickened, and he pulled at her hand to get her to walk faster.

"Where are we going?" she asked as she moved faster alongside him.

"I know a place where we'll be safe, where you'll be safe."

"Paul, I'm scared," JoAnna said as her hand broke free of his and fell to her side. He stopped and looked back at her and could tell she was terrified. It pained him to see her so frightened, but he knew they didn't have much time. When he walked back to her, she thrust herself into his arms and buried her face in the crook of his neck.

"Oh Paul, what's going on? What are you not telling me?" she said as she tilted her head back and looked into his eyes.

"Where *are* we?"

28

As Paul and JoAnna hurried down the cobblestone street, she eyed the dark houses around them. She didn't understand why he was in such a hurry. What did he know? What would happen to them if they didn't get inside?

A roadside motel sat at the end of the street. "Is that where we're going?" she asked. He was staring at the motel, relieved to have found it.

"It can be anything you want, Jo. Just close your eyes and imagine it. The Swamp Fox Inn, or anything place you want it to be. Any motel you can remember."

JoAnna frowned. "What? The Swamp Fox Inn?"

"Anything, Jo. Just picture it in your mind."

JoAnna didn't understand but closed her eyes and tried to imagine a motel. When she opened them, the motel had transformed into the Swamp Fox Inn. A yellow light spilling out of the small window near the office door reminded her of Cooper.

"I'm scared, Paul. I don't want this."

"Try something else, Jo. We don't have much time."

When JoAnna reopened her eyes, the Swamp Fox Inn had transformed into the motel her family had stayed at during their summer vacations at Carolina Beach. They walked across the street and once inside a room, Paul locked the door behind them. A lamp spilled dim light onto the nightstand between the two double beds and when JoAnna saw the room she realized it looked just like the one she had stayed in with her parents when she was little. The same sailboat painting hung on the wall and the bed covers carried the same seashell-patterned print.

Paul breathed a sigh of relief as they sat down on the edge of the bed. "Don't leave this room tonight for any reason, Jo. Promise me that." He put his arm around her and felt her shaking, but knew she would be okay if she obeyed his instructions. He didn't want her to see what would happen at sunrise.

"What will we do in the morning?" JoAnna asked. "I wish you would tell me what's going on."

"I've told you all I can tell you for now, Jo. I'm sorry."

JoAnna put her head on his shoulder. "I'm so tired. I just want to lie down and feel your arms around me. Can we do that? I don't want to think about tomorrow or anything else." The room tilted and yawed, and she felt dizzy. Before she could say another word, she fell backwards onto the bed fast asleep. Paul pulled her legs onto the bed and put a pillow underneath her head, then laid down next to her.

When JoAnna woke up, hazy-gray daylight filled the room. She sat up in bed, rubbed her eyes and tried to focus on the wall in front of her. The sailboat painting now hung at an odd angle. At first this didn't alarm her, but when she saw the torn strips of wallpaper and the broken vanity mirror, she knew something was wrong. Then she looked beside her and saw that Paul was gone.

The room looked completely different. The carpet had long since rotted away, replaced by weeds sprouting through cracks in the floor. The table and chairs by the window were lying on their sides and a large fern was growing out of a hole in the concrete. A grimy film covered the bare window panes. JoAnna got out of bed, stepped over to the window and looked through the murky glass at the outlines of the buildings across the street. When she turned around and saw the empty bed again, she felt a pang of heartache.

JoAnna exhaled and looked at the empty bed. She didn't want to admit it to herself, but there was no use in denying the truth any longer. Yes, Izzy had made good on their bargain but there had never been an agreement on how long Paul would get to stay with her. Maybe last night was all she would get. She pressed herself against the door and slowly slid down until she was sitting on the cold concrete. Then she started to cry.

JoAnna sat on the floor, her arms across her knees and cried for what seemed like hours. Izzy had taken advantage of her and now she was in her debt. But what that debt was she had no idea. But she knew one thing, and that was if one night with Paul was all she would get, then the only thing left for her to do now was to get out of Summerland. If she could get back to the main road, she could flag down a passing car and beg for a ride back to civilization. Anywhere would be better than here. As for paying Izzy, she would just have to deal with that when the time came.

Outside the motel, the town looked abandoned and in disrepair. Some buildings had lost their roofs, others had broken windows and overgrown lawns. Just as the night before, there were no signs of life anywhere. Then she noticed the position of the sun and realized that it was close to setting. It wasn't morning, but rather late afternoon. She had apparently slept away most of the day.

Once JoAnna retraced her steps and made her way back to the boardwalk, she walked towards the amusement park but her pace slowed as she approached the miniature golf course. She could see the rides and the Midway, but something was wrong. Weeds and underbrush covered the golf course, and beyond the empty game booths she could see the Merry-Go-Round, its horses frozen in time on their mounts. Some of them lay next to the ride, half buried in the dirt. Past the Ferris wheel sat the Pavilion, its roof collapsed into the second floor. In place of the Skee-Ball machines, long strings of graffiti covered the back wall.

JoAnna could not fathom the appearance of the park. She had no idea what was going on but as much as it terrified her to think about it, she knew the only way out was through the park to the main gate. She wasn't sure which way to go, but she stepped off the boardwalk anyway, hoping that she would be able to find the gate.

The sky lift poles, now devoid of their cables and cars, rose into the air at even intervals across the park. When she looked across at the roller coaster, its rails rusted dark from years of disuse, she caught a movement out of the corner of her eye. She stopped but didn't see anything at first. But she was certain it was there, and despite her fear knew she had to find out what it was.

Moving down the row of booths, she came to the Tilt-a-Whirl, its colorful roof now lying across the cars. A few moments passed, and then the faint *clank* of metal on metal broke the surrounding silence.

"Is someone there?" she said. "Hello?" There was no answer. She walked down the row until she came to a small trailer that had once sold funnel cakes. It sat on steel hubs and leaned to one side, the glass gone from the windows. Faded images of funnel cakes, washed out by years of sun exposure covered the side of the trailer. JoAnna put her hand against the sheet metal, then leaned out and looked around the corner.

The sound was coming from a small cinderblock shed sitting close to the rusted skeleton of the Ferris wheel. The shed was no bigger than the trailer she was standing next to but it was in better condition. There was still glass in the two small windows on the front of the shed, but years of exposure to the weather had fogged them over. JoAnna closed her eyes and took a deep breath, trying to find the courage to approach the shed. Then she heard the sound again.

Clank clank…

Through the grime coated window, she saw something move inside the shed. This was her chance. Now was the time to find out what was going on. Whoever was in the shed could tell her about Summerland. Then she thought about Paul. Maybe it was him making the noise.

JoAnna stepped away from the funnel cake trailer. Her desire to find out what was going on overruled the fear stinging the back of her neck. When she stepped up to the shed door, she heard another *clank* and then the sound of something falling to the floor. A low, muffled grunt followed. Gathering her wits, she pulled opened the door and peered into the shadowy interior of the shed just as a scream clawed its way up her throat.

29

The creature in the old brown overalls turned and looked at JoAnna as she stood in the doorway. When she saw his face, she put her hand over her mouth and took a step backwards. She knew the face of the man but couldn't place him. The burn marks and disfigured skin made it hard for her to remember where she had seen him before.

Pain flashed across the man's face as he rose to his feet. His overalls, weathered and torn in several places, carried stains of oil and dried paint. One arm hung limp at his side and the other hand held an old rag. When he saw the look of recognition on JoAnna's face he raised the rag in front of his face, then looked down at his feet in shame.

JoAnna dropped her hand from her mouth and placed it across her heart when she realized who she was looking at. The last time she had seen him was during her first night at the Swamp Fox Inn.

"Cooper…?"

Cooper didn't respond. He held the rag closer to his face and turned as if trying to hide behind it. He seemed both afraid of JoAnna and embarrassed by his face.

"Cooper, is that you? Do you remember me? I'm JoAnna. JoAnna Stedford."

Cooper dropped the rag to his side and looked at JoAnna. His embarrassment ebbed once he realized she was no longer afraid of him.

"I… I am Cooper," he said, the ruined flesh around his mouth slurring his words. His eyes returned to the ground.

"What are you doing here, Cooper? Where *are* we? What is this place?"

Cooper didn't respond as he stepped backwards and sat down on a wooden crate. He let out a sigh as if sitting down eased the pain.

"You told her I scared you," Cooper said. JoAnna watched as his tongue moved over his dry, cracked lips. When he closed his mouth, she could still see a few of his teeth though the hole in his upper lip.

"I told her you scared me? Who? Who did I tell?"

Cooper paused for a moment, wary of saying another word, then finally said, "The old witch that lives in the house outside of town. She punished me for what I did to you." When Cooper said this, a line of saliva trailed down his chin from the hole in his lip. He reached up and wiped at it with his good arm. When he finished wiping his chin, he put the old rag in his other hand and JoAnna watched as the fingers curled around it. Then he shifted his weight and winced in pain.

She thought back to the night at Izzy's house and how she had told Izzy about being scared by the night man at the Swamp Fox Inn. She remembered Izzy's words and the look of anger that had flashed across her face.

I have something planned for him...

With a heavy heart, JoAnna said, "Oh, Cooper. What happened to you?"

"She made sure I paid for what I did to you. She burned up the office while I was asleep. But I was only trying to help you that first night, to tell you to get out of town." Cooper reached for his rag and wiped his chin again.

JoAnna remembered the flame marks around the office door of the Swamp Fox Inn. She placed her hand across her chest and looked a poor Cooper sitting there on the wooden crate, the skin on his face and hands burned so badly they looked like shoe leather. Cooper reached up and adjusted his ragged hat, then looked down at the ground as a bolt of pain rocketed through his body.

JoAnna felt another wave of guilt wash over her. Even though Cooper had scared her, and Lydia had called him the town creep, being burned alive and left to live in an old shed in this abandoned amusement park seemed to her to be a particularly cruel form of punishment. And why would Izzy feel the need to punish him? JoAnna wondered what made her so special to Izzy to warrant that kind of response. And if Izzy could do this to someone, then she was not the kind, homespun woman that she had appeared to be. JoAnna thought about Izzy standing by her stove wearing a duck apron and wondered if it all been an illusion. What did she really look like? And if Izzy could burn Cooper alive, JoAnna didn't want to think about what she could do to someone that thought they could get out of their end of a deal.

Outside, the sun hung low in the trees as JoAnna looked down at Cooper sitting on the wooden crate. She wanted to get out of the amusement park and back to the main road before it got dark, but she knew Cooper had the answers to some of her questions.

"You're special," Cooper said as he leaned over and rested his good arm on his knee, grimacing in pain. A small ball of spittle dripped out of the hole in his lip and onto the dirty brown material covering his legs. He looked down at it and then used his rag to wipe his chin again.

Cooper knew that his punishment wasn't because he scared a young woman at the Swamp Fox Inn, one who was vulnerable and traveling alone. He knew he was sitting on the old wooden crate, his skin blistered red, because he had scared a very special young woman, one that Isabelle Pearl had plans for. She had not only burned him from head to toe but had also sentenced him to be the caretaker of this hellish amusement park. And now the young girl that had caused him all this agony, and the condemnation of his soul, was standing in front of him. But he knew that any anger towards her would result in more punishment, and that it would be far worse than anything he had ever felt before. Isabelle Pearl would know if he mistreated JoAnna and she would make her displeasure known in a most horrific manner. Perhaps her next punishment would be to peel the ruined skin right off his bones.

JoAnna squatted down eye level with Cooper. "Why am I so special, Cooper? Why would Isabelle Pearl take up for me like this?"

Cooper's lips parted, showing his yellow teeth. "She protects you because you carry his child." Cooper ran his tongue across his lips again and then looked down at his feet, certain that something horrible would happen to him in the next few moments. He coughed and winced from the pain, knowing that it was a prelude to what was coming if he kept talking.

Anger flashed hot across JoAnna's face. "You're a liar," she hissed. "How could you possibly know that?"

Cooper ignored her and continued to stare at the dirt floor of the shed, certain that Izzy's next round of punishment was only moments away.

"Nothing is free," Cooper said as he shifted his weight. "Nothing is ever free with that woman."

"You're a liar…" JoAnna repeated, but this time her voice lacked conviction. Part of her wanted to believe Cooper, but a flicker of doubt remained.

Cooper knew there was no need to argue with her, and he was fearful to say anything else. He knew she would find out soon enough that he was telling her the truth. He turned his head and looked at JoAnna, then he looked past her at the dark sky beyond. The sun had gone down, and he knew what was about to happen. When JoAnna noticed Cooper looking past her and out into the park, she looked over her shoulder.

All of a sudden, light and sound exploded around them as the amusement park roared to life. It happened in an instant. Startled, JoAnna stood up and stepped through the door of the shed to watch the scene unfolding around her. Gone were all the ruined rides and collapsed game booths. The rusted hulk of the roller coaster was now functional, its frame lit with thousands colorful lights blinking in unison. Then she heard the familiar sound of the pipe organ from the Merry-Go-Round. All the game booths were standing erect while invisible hands once again played the games. And then, just like the night before, the sky erupted in fireworks.

JoAnna turned and looked at the shed, but Cooper had already closed the door. She stepped up and slapped it with her hand, then twisted the doorknob. "Cooper! Cooper, open the door!" But he didn't respond.

Stepping away from the shed, JoAnna watched the roller coaster climb the rails and roar down the track. Beside it, the Tilt-a-Whirl turned on its axis, its rotating cars bathed in the yellow neon glow of the overhead lights. Disgusted, she turned and ran in the direction of the front gate. She remembered the ticket booth she and Paul had passed when they entered the park the night before and she knew if she could find that booth, the road beyond led to the main highway. But as she ran down the row of game booths along the Midway, she realized that either her memory was failing her or the park was arranged differently than it had been the night before. Every time she turned and ran down a row it led her back to the same place.

JoAnna stopped to gather her breath next to a fortune telling machine. A Genie with eyes glowing green stared at her from behind the glass. When she leaned against the booth to catch her breath and calm down, the Genie's head came to life. His mouth opened and closed, then a bell dinged and a card fell into a slot on the front of the machine. She didn't want to reach for the card, but she had to know what it said. She reached for it, then read the small print.

There is no escape…

JoAnna took a step backwards but the Genie's eyes followed her as she moved. She looked down at the card again and back at the Genie, then ran down the closest row of game booths. When she reached the end, she turned down another row, but after repeating this several more times she realized that the words on the card were true. There was no escape. Every row led her back to the same place.

Refusing to give up, JoAnna took off down another row. As she passed the arm-wrestling machine, she stopped and watched the metal arm move back and forth as it wrestled with an invisible opponent. When the arm slammed down in victory, a bell rang and a row of lights flashed across the top of the machine. She grimaced at the sight of it, then moved away from the machine and continued down the row.

The sky lift hung above her, but unlike all the other rides in the park was not moving. When she stopped at the wheelhouse to survey the ride, a latch popped on one of the cars and the door drifted open. Against her better judgement, she walked through the gate and got in the car knowing her only choice was to get in and see where it would take her, or go back through the park to try to find the entrance. Once in the car, the door closed and the sky lift came to life. She watched her surroundings rotate around her as the car traveled through the wheelhouse before starting its climb to the first pole.

The cars in front and behind her were empty. As she rose above the park, she tried to see out over the huge body of water lying beyond the boardwalk but the starless sky blended with the black water to erase the horizon. At the end of the boardwalk, past a large dark patch of sand dunes, she could see the Wild West town, its single street lit by gas lamps hanging from posts. In the center of the town sat the old saloon advertised on the billboard.

A sudden metallic noise startled JoAnna as the car moved past the first support pole. Looking down into the park, she saw Cooper walk out of his shed while the empty rides whirred around him.

30

Once off the sky lift, JoAnna stood in the shadows next to the wheelhouse and knew she had been a fool to trust Isabelle Pearl. Yes, Isabelle had kept her end of the bargain and returned Paul, but now it was obvious that one night with him was all she was going to get. But she realized that Isabelle had never promised otherwise. As much as she tried to deny it, they had never agreed on the length of time Paul would get to be with her. Now she was trapped in a hellish place, struggling to keep a hold of her wits and unsure if she was dead, alive, or somewhere in between.

JoAnna touched her abdomen and thought again about what Cooper had said about her carrying Izzy's grandchild. Tears filled her eyes. Could it be true? Was that why Izzy had told her she was special? She thought about Cooper's ruined body and the price he had paid for scaring her. Even though she didn't want to admit it to herself, this seemed to prove that what Cooper had said was true. Why else would Izzy care about her so much that she would do such a thing to him?

Feeling weak on her feet, JoAnna leaned against the wall of the wheelhouse. Deep down inside she knew Cooper was right. But why her? Lydia had told her that Isabelle's son enjoyed many of the women that came to their house in search of his mother's services. He had even taken Lydia. It just didn't make any sense to her why Izzy chose her to be the mother of this child. It had to be her price for having Paul returned to her.

JoAnna knew she had to get moving. There had to be a way out of Summerland and there had to be a way out of her deal with Izzy. She stepped away from the wheelhouse and walked over to an adjoining street that led into the town. Walking through the puddles of light from the gas lamps, her pace quickened as she moved past the small houses that lined the street. At first there were no signs of life in anywhere, but then came a sound in the distance. She waited for a few seconds and then heard it again, a high-pitched whine that echoed all around her.

A train whistle... she thought.

As she continued down the street, she heard the whistle again and knew she was getting close. She could hear the chugging and hissing of the engine, and when she got to the end of the street, she looked across to the town square and saw the empty train station. Gas lamps hung from poles on each side of the station and illuminated several rows of empty benches sitting on the platform above the tracks.

Suddenly the whistle sounded again, so loudly that JoAnna raised her hands to her ears to cover them. When the engine emerged from the tree line, she stepped into the alcove of a nearby store to hide herself. She wanted to know more about the train before she rushed to the station for help, so she stood in the shadows and watched as it approached the station while puffing steam into the night air. Followed by a coal tender, three passenger cars and a caboose, the engine pulled to the station and stopped. Steam erupted in a long burst from underneath as the unseen engineer released pressure from the boiler. Dim light emanated from the windows of the passenger cars and JoAnna could see shapes through the glass. A wave of goose bumps erupted across her arms as she watched the shapes move about in the cars.

At first it seemed as if no one was going to get off the train, but then the doors opened with a hiss and the passengers started filing off the train and onto the platform. JoAnna wanted to rush to the station, but then chided herself for assuming that the people getting off the train would offer her any kind of help.

JoAnna watched as the passengers ambled about on the platform under the yellow light of the gas lamps. Then the whistle sounded, followed by the slow *chug chug* of the engine as the train pulled away. Once clear of the station it blew its whistle again, then disappeared in a haze of shimmering light.

JoAnna watched as the passengers dispersed, moving in all directions away from the station onto the small cobblestone streets connecting the town square. When a group of them ambled past her hiding spot in the alcove, they didn't see her standing in the shadows. Suddenly she realized that she recognized one of the faces. When she looked again, it was all she could do to keep silent and not alert the group to her presence. She took a step backwards until she felt the cold glass press against her back, then brought her hand to her mouth to stifle a gasp as she watched her mother walk by the alcove.

JoAnna stood frozen in the darkness, her mind racing. Until this point, she had known Summerland wasn't a normal little town. The amusement park had proven that, but now she was struggling with the realization that Summerland was far worse than anything she could have imagined. The fact that her mother had just walked past the alcove was all the proof she needed to know that something was horribly wrong.

She couldn't hold back the tears and did her best to muffle the sobs as tears traced lines down her face. Now she realized why her mother hadn't returned any of her calls over the past few days. Something terrible had happened. The proof, in the form of her mother's soul, had just ambled past her on the sidewalk.

As JoAnna stood in the dark corner of the alcove, she realized her mother really was gone, and whatever had just walked by was not someone she could run to for comfort. She remembered how Paul had told her that the longer she was in Summerland the more she would be able to see. That had to be why she had been able to see the souls walking past the alcove.

Despair pooled in her abdomen. What had she done? What kind of horrible deal had she made with Wicked Izzy? Was she nothing more than just another wayward soul wandering the streets of this hellish little town? Was she dead or alive? She placed her hand on her abdomen and thought about what Cooper had told her. If she was really carrying Wicked Izzy's grandchild then she had to be alive and just trapped in this town. And if that were true, there had to be an escape. There had to be some way out for both her and her child.

31

JoAnna pushed away from the lamppost and made her way down the street. Once through the alleyway and back on the boardwalk, she could see the neon glow of the amusement park beyond the rooftops. Just as she stepped out of the alleyway, movement down the boardwalk caught her eyes. She ducked into the shadows and waited to see whatever it was coming her way.

JoAnna watched as the figure ambled along, disappearing in the long patches of darkness between the gas lamps. She held her body completely still, afraid that the slightest movement would give her away but as the person got closer, she saw the long hair and recognized Lydia's face immediately. She stepped out of the shadows and rushed to her.

"Lydia... Is that you?"

Lydia didn't respond. Instead, she stopped and slowly turned her head in JoAnna's direction. She stood motionless on the boardwalk, her hair lifting off her shoulders in the breeze, but there was no recognition in her eyes. JoAnna studied her for a few moments, trying to figure out what was different about her friend. She wondered why Lydia didn't embrace her. They were friends so why was she acting so strangely?

"Lydia?"

Lydia's hair loitered around her face before a breeze caught it and exposed her eyes. They were as black as the water behind her. JoAnna gasped and fought the urge to run, but then she thought that maybe her friend needed help. She took a step forward but noticed that Lydia's eyes didn't move. They just stared blankly past her.

"Oh Lydia, what happened to you? Did she do this to you?" she asked, but Lydia didn't respond.

JoAnna took a step backwards and thought about Lydia's price for having Jacob returned to her. Could this be it? But what exactly had Izzy taken from her? When she looked at Lydia again it dawned on her that her body seemed to be a lifeless shell. Had Izzy taken her soul? This was the only answer that made any sense. Izzy had returned Jacob for a few days and then sentenced Lydia's soulless body to wander in Summerland forever. As JoAnna thought about this, Lydia slowly turned her head and resumed her shuffle down the boardwalk.

Realizing Lydia couldn't help her find her way out of Summerland, JoAnna watched her friend's body as it walked away and disappeared into another patch of darkness between the gas lamps. Then she turned and moved quickly down the boardwalk in the opposite direction, retracing the steps she had taken earlier in the day. As she walked, she looked out over the dark, eerie ocean to her left and then at the small houses that lined the other side of the boardwalk. The faint sound of the organ called out to her as she approached the miniature golf course.

Moving quickly through the greens, JoAnna walked past a small windmill sitting over one of the holes. Across from the windmill stood a large clown with yellow pants and a striped red and white shirt. The last hole of the course was between the clown's feet.

Once out of the golf course, she moved past several food trailers painted with images of ice cream cones, slices of pizza and cotton candy. She went past the Merry-Go-Round and stopped when she saw Cooper's shed. The amusement park around her was alive with sounds and lights, but just as the night before seemed deserted.

When she saw the closed door of the shed JoAnna wondered if Cooper was still inside. Could that be where he lived? She walked up and banged on the door several times but there was no response.

"Cooper!" Trying to raise her voice over the organ music, she yelled out again. "Cooper, open the door!" When he didn't respond, she slapped the door again with the palm of her hand.

"What do you want?" Cooper said, his garbled words coming from behind her.

JoAnna turned and saw him standing in the glow of the neon lights, his burned skin the color of caramel. He worked the hole in his lip with his tongue and then looked down at his feet in embarrassment. Despite her revulsion, JoAnna moved closer so that she could talk to him over the surrounding noise. The smell from his blistered skin overwhelmed her senses, and she fought the urge to cover her mouth with her hand. She needed Cooper's help, and she knew that giving him the impression that his appearance sickened her was not in her best interests.

"Cooper, what is this place? Where are we?"

"Summerland," he said. He reached into his pocket with his good hand and removed his handkerchief, dabbed his mouth with it and then returned it to his pocket. Then he coughed and his entire body shook.

"This is her place."

"Why is it empty? Where is everyone? All the rides are moving but no one's on them."

Cooper looked at JoAnna as if he didn't understand what she was saying. "Empty?" he said as he looked over at the Merry-Go-Round, its horses moving up and down as it turned.

"Yes, empty. We're the only ones here. And in the daytime this place looks abandoned."

Cooper looked back at JoAnna, his tongue playing against his bare teeth as he tried once again to understand what she was saying.

"You can't see them?" he finally asked.

"See who?" JoAnna said.

"You can't see the souls?"

"No, I can't see anyone but you, Cooper."

Cooper shook his head. "They're everywhere. This place is full of them." He lifted his good arm and pointed at the Midway. JoAnna heard a bell ring in one of the booths, signaling that someone had just won something. "The games... It goes on all night."

Their heads turned when they heard the clank of the roller coaster climbing the rails behind them. "This is her place," he said. "You will see what she wants you to see."

Disbelief bloomed on JoAnna's face. Cooper had to be making this up, she thought. He knew she was scared and was just trying to make it worse. But she remembered that Paul had told her the same thing.

"I can see you, Cooper. Why can I see you?"

"Because I am not one of them. I am... I am *alive*. I am being punished so I can never leave like they can."

She watched as Cooper's eyes fell to the ground. "I can never leave," he repeated, his words slurred. A small bit of spittle dripped from the hole in his lip and ran down his chin, but he made no effort to wipe it away. JoAnna felt a rush of pity. This was all her fault.

"Oh Cooper, I'm so sorry…"

"They wait their turn and then they leave." Cooper's eyes traveled back to the roller coaster as he watched it rumble down the first hill and then rocket around the track, the bright neon lights along the rails contrasting sharply against the black sky.

At first JoAnna didn't believe him. Whatever kind of place this was it certainly wasn't an amusement park full of the souls of the dead. That was the most ridiculous thing she had ever heard. But when she thought about Paul, the passengers on the train, and Lydia's empty body walking on the boardwalk, everything started to make sense.

"Cooper, I need to get out of here. How can I do that? Can you tell me?"

Cooper shifted his weight and winced in pain.

"You will leave when it suits her."

"That's bullshit, Cooper. I'm leaving tonight. Just point me in the direction of the gate."

Cooper shook his head. "You will leave when it suits her."

Behind them the Tilt-a-Whirl slowed and came to a stop. They both turned and watched as the restraint arms rose in the cars. After a few minutes, the arms went down and the cars started moving again.

"Can you see them?" she asked. Cooper shifted his weight to his other leg and then reached into his pocket for his handkerchief. But instead of wiping his mouth with it, he raised it and wiped his eyes. After a long pause, he looked down at the ground.

"I can see everything. It's what she wants."

JoAnna tried to imagine what the amusement park looked like through Cooper's eyes. Then she turned to look at him. Another rush of pity flushed through her. How could she have caused this to happen to this poor man?

"Who is she? How does she do all of this?" JoAnna asked as she waved an arm at the surrounding rides. "How does Isabelle Pearl do all of this?" She watched the color drain out of Cooper's face and knew she had hit home with her question. Now maybe she would find out the truth.

"Her name is not Isabelle. She just uses that, but it is not her real name." Cooper winced as a sharp blade of pain cut through his abdomen. Pity welled up inside of JoAnna as she watched Cooper suffer at her expense. He wiped his forehead and then his mouth before returning his handkerchief to his pocket.

"Then what is her real name?"

"Her name is..." Cooper caught himself and stopped short of telling JoAnna the real name of Isabelle Pearl. He knew what would happen if he did.

"I... I cannot say her name."

"Then tell me *what* she is. You don't have to tell me her name."

Cooper's eyes burned with fear as they met JoAnna's. She hated to push him for answers but she had to know the truth about Isabelle Pearl.

"Tell me, Cooper. Please tell me." She watched as the fear in Cooper's eyes flared even brighter.

"She is the wife," he finally said. Then he raised his handkerchief to his mouth and coughed into it, his chest rattling beneath his dirty overalls.

JoAnna's mouth dropped open. "Whose wife? Cooper, who are you talking about?"

Cooper realized he had said too much. His face contorted as the pain rocketed through his body. He knew if he kept talking that it would be the end for him, but it would be a relief from the agony of living inside the shell of his ruined skin.

"She is the wife," repeated Cooper. "They call her..."

Just as Cooper was about to tell JoAnna the name, a sharp bolt of pain electrified his body. She watched as he raised a hand to his face.

"No! I'm sorry. I'm sorry!" Cooper tilted his head back and looked up in the air. Then he placed his fingers in his mouth and hooked them over his bottom row of teeth. JoAnna watched as he pulled his mouth open until she heard the bones start to crack. A sickening pop followed as he ripped his entire lower jaw free from his head.

JoAnna screamed and backed away as the blood poured out of Cooper's face. Bile surged up her throat as she looked at Cooper standing there holding his lower jaw in his hand. His eyes were ablaze with terror. He looked down at the hand holding his jaw, then he dropped to his knees and fell forward onto the dirt.

Suddenly a hot wind roared through the amusement park. JoAnna shielded her eyes from the blowing sand as a dust devil rose and consumed Cooper's body. Then the wind stopped and when the dust devil disappeared, he was gone.

In an instant, JoAnna made her decision. She turned and ran past the Merry-Go-Round and then down a row of game booths towards the boardwalk. If she could get there, maybe she could make her way to the beach and to freedom.

When she reached the boardwalk, she ran to the railing and looked out at the dark ocean beyond. The neon lights from the amusement park cast a shadow onto the sand below her, and even though she could not see far enough to see the edge of the water she could hear the waves lapping at the shoreline. This was her chance, she thought. This was her chance to escape from Summerland.

"JoAnna…"

Her entire body stiffened when she heard the voice behind her. It wasn't Paul's voice, but rather a woman's voice and even though she recognized it immediately, she couldn't bring herself to turn around.

"JoAnna…" came the voice again.

JoAnna closed her eyes and dropped her chin to her chest. When she turned around and saw the woman standing only a few feet away, tears rolled down her face and she had to grasp the railing to keep from passing out.

"Oh JoAnna…" Maxine Stedford said as she raised her arms to her daughter.

32

JoAnna stood motionless on the boardwalk, the sound of the waves behind her barely audible over the sound of the rides. She couldn't bring herself to reach out to her mother.

"My dear JoAnna... Come to me." Maxine's voice was clear and inviting. JoAnna felt the love she had for her mother pull at her heart, and the feeling was strong enough to make her want to take a step forward. But at the last moment, fear overwhelmed her and she stayed against the handrail. After watching Cooper rip his own jaw from his head, she knew the image of her mother might be a trick.

JoAnna wiped her eyes with both of her hands and tried to grasp the idea that the ghost of her mother was standing right in front of her. She drew in a deep breath and tried to gather her strength. Her mother's arms were still outstretched and when she couldn't take it anymore, she gave into her love and raced into them. Relief flooded through her body when they embraced.

"Oh Mom, I've missed you so much," she said as she pulled back and looked into her mother's eyes. They were soft and peaceful in the neon light. Maxine smiled and pushed the hair away from her daughter's face.

"I've missed you too, sweetie."

"Where are we, mother? What is this place? What is going on?"

The expression on Maxine's face darkened as she looked into JoAnna's eyes.

"I died the night that I came to get you. The abandoned town... I just didn't understand what was going on and then there was a man in the road. I swerved to miss him and that's when I drove into the canal. My body is still there but my soul is here, confined to this place. The Summerland. You must leave while you can, JoAnna."

"*The* Summerland? What are you talking about, Mom? This is just a town."

"No, JoAnna, this is not just a town. It is full of the souls of those who died a violent death. You cannot see them because you are not one of them but they're all around us. They stay here until a loved one makes a deal for their return."

"Isabelle Pearl..." JoAnna looked at her mother. Everything was beginning to make sense now.

Maxine nodded her head and then looked over her shoulder at the amusement park. Her eyes darted from side to side as they followed the souls that only she could see. JoAnna looked past her mother at the empty amusement park, her eyes wide with fear.

"Why am I here, Mom? I want to leave but I don't know how."

"She has a special plan for you, JoAnna. You will bear her son's child. She will let you leave when the time comes."

Maxine placed her hands on JoAnna's cheeks. Instead of being warm, they were cold and clammy and when JoAnna felt them she took a step backwards. Then Maxine started coughing, her chest heaving as if she were choking. Suddenly swamp water poured from her mouth, and just as JoAnna was about to reach out to try to help, her mother's ghost faded away.

JoAnna couldn't take any more of Summerland, or *the* Summerland, or whatever her mother had called it. And she had had her fill of the amusement park and the boardwalk. She turned quickly and ran down the boardwalk steps to the sand dunes below. Once on the sand, she ran towards the water, then stopped to look back at the park. Disbelief bloomed on her face.

The amusement park was full of people. They were walking along the Midway and some were at the booths playing the games. She could see the Ferris wheel turning, its bright neon lights blinking in rhythm as it rotated, each car full of riders. Dark silhouettes of people moved along the boardwalk, some walking hand in hand with a companion, others alone.

Across the park, JoAnna could see the Pavilion, its bottom floor now full of people dancing and twirling about. The Tilt-a-Whirl and the other rides were also full of riders, and the miniature golf course had players on each green.

Frightened at the sight of all the souls in the park, JoAnna turned made her way across the dunes towards the sound of the waves breaking in the darkness. When the sand hardened under her feet and she knew she was close to the water, she looked back at the amusement park again. Some of the people standing at the railing were pointing in her direction. She stepped backwards a few feet and bent down to touch the film of water at her feet. It was warm to the touch.

Trying to decide which way to go, JoAnna looked down the beach and saw a splash of hazy light in the distance. Could it be another town? She looked back at the boardwalk, then at the light down the beach and made her choice. She took off towards the distant lights, but after she walked for a few minutes and the lights started to come into focus, she realized something was wrong. Tears welled in her eyes as she remembered the card from the fortune telling machine.

There is no escape...

Sitting in front of her was the same amusement park she had just escaped from, its rides rotating in the wash of neon lights. The sounds of bells and organ music filled the air, and she could even smell the hint of popcorn. Feeling completely defeated, she crossed her arms against her chest and turned to look out across the dark ocean. The Genie had told her the truth. There really was no escape. She knew if she turned and ran back down the beach, she would just arrive at the same place again, and see the same rides and boardwalk. Disheartened, she sat down on the sand and stared out into the black ocean in front of her.

JoAnna wasn't sure if minutes or hours had passed when she finally rose from the sand and walked to the edge of the water. When it washed over her feet, it felt warm and inviting and seemed to beckon to her. She gave into the mysterious pull and took a few more steps into the water until she was in up to her knees. Just as she was about to push into deeper water, a voice called out from behind her.

"JoAnna!"

JoAnna turned and saw someone standing at the edge of the water. Thinking it had to be some sort of trick, she almost turned back towards the water to continue on, but then the voice called out again.

"JoAnna! Stop!"

The second time she heard the voice she recognized it immediately. It was Paul's voice. She turned and pushed her knees through the water, quickening her pace as she moved into shallow water. Once on the beach, she ran to his arms.

"Oh Paul!" she said as their bodies met. "I missed you. Where did you go? Why did you leave me in the motel?"

Paul looked down at JoAnna, her face bathed in the light from the park behind them. "What were you doing in the water?" he said, ignoring her question about the motel.

"I wanted to escape, but there is no way out of here. I can't find the gate we came through, and when I ran down the beach it just led me back to the same place. I figured the only thing left to do was to just go into the water. I thought that maybe killing myself was the only way out of here."

Paul smiled. "That's what saved you, Jo. The only thing Isabelle can't do is stop you from killing yourself. You're too important to her so she changed her mind and instead of just letting you have me for one day, we can now be together forever. You're the only person she has ever changed the terms of a deal for, Jo. That's how special you are to her."

When JoAnna heard this, she hugged Paul tightly. His body felt warm and when their lips met, she felt the world around them slip away. When they parted, she looked into his eyes and then at the amusement park.

"We can leave now, Jo." When Paul said this, he took JoAnna by the hand and led her across the dunes and back to the amusement park.

33

Melissa sat in the small booth of the diner staring through the window at the street outside. Most of the booths and tables around her were empty, but the counter had several patrons sitting on the stools sipping coffee and eating breakfast. She said his name again, this time under her breath so no one could hear her. A few minutes before she had drawn a few stares when she had said his name aloud. But she loved him more than anything in the world and it was hard to contain her emotions.

She took a sip of her coffee and looked out the window again at the vacant parking lot of the small motel sitting next to the diner. She was tired from driving all night and at this point all she wanted was a warm bed and a few hours of sleep. But she dismissed the thought. She would order breakfast and then get back in her car and start driving again. Driving was the only time she felt any peace and even if she did rent a room at the motel, she knew she would only toss and turn. That's how it had been every night for the past two months.

The hot coffee comforted her as she replayed the events of that terrible night two months ago. She had lost count of how many times she had done this since getting in the car last night and each time the result was the same. No matter how she tried to skew the events of that fateful night, she couldn't help but blame herself for what had happened.

"More coffee?" The soft female voice jolted her out of her reverie. She nodded and pushed her cup over to the edge of the table.

"Are you ready to order?"

Melissa looked down at her cup. "Um, in a few minutes. I'd like to drink this cup first. I mean, if that's okay."

The server smiled. "Just take your time, girlfriend. No hurry at all." She took her coffee pot and disappeared into the kitchen. Melissa watched as the swinging doors separating the kitchen from the dining area swung back and forth and then came to a stop.

Her mind wandered again. Why had she asked him to go out? It was late that night, and the weather was terrible. It had been raining hard since early that morning and the roads were awful. But she had a craving and had bribed him with the promise of sex if he would just make an ice cream run. He had agreed immediately, just like he always did when she promised sex, and when he walked to the door to leave, she had no idea that it was the last time she would ever see him. When the tractor-trailer T-boned him after running a red light, the state trooper told her that her fiancée had died instantly.

The last few weeks had been the hardest weeks of her life. Instead of getting better she found herself slipping deeper and deeper into depression. Last night she had finally reached the point where she could no longer stand the idea of staying in her lonely apartment. She had packed an overnight bag, took what cash she could out of the ATM, and started driving. She had left Asheville just after sunset and had driven all night. Now she found herself sitting in a diner in the small town of Solomon.

Melissa thought about him again and how he had been everything in the world to her. Her parents had died three years ago, both shot to death when they had surprised a burglar after returning home late one night. Learning to live without them had been hard enough, but she had eventually gained the strength to put it all behind her. And then when visiting a friend from college just over a year ago she had met Stephen, and after one look into his eyes had known that he was the one she had been waiting for all her life. Now he was gone, and it was all because of her.

The server returned with a pot of coffee. As she poured, she noticed the empty creamer dish. "Let me get you some more cream," she said after she finished filling the cup.

Melissa smiled. "That would be nice. I really can't drink coffee without it."

The server nodded her head. "I hear ya. I just don't know how some people do that." She disappeared and returned a few moments later with a handful of small plastic creamers and deposited them in the dish next to the napkin dispenser.

"Are you ready to order?"

Melissa glanced down at the paper place mat underneath her cup that served double duty as a place mat and a menu.

"I guess I'll have two eggs scrambled, bacon, home fries and white toast. And maybe a side order of gravy and biscuits." She smiled, trying to hide her embarrassment. "I've been driving all night," she said as she felt her cheeks flush. The server smiled as she wrote on her order pad.

"Driving all night? Where are you from?"

"I'm from Asheville."

The server stopped writing on her pad for a moment and looked at Melissa. "That's all the way on the other side of the state. That's a long drive."

"Yes, it is," Melissa said.

The server frowned. "Are you okay?"

"I'm fine. I'm just going through a rough time right now. Driving seems to help. It beats sitting around my little apartment in Asheville thinking about..." She stopped short and looked out the window.

"Did he leave you for someone else?" replied the server. She was a young girl herself and knew the signs of heartache all too well.

"Oh no, it was nothing like that," Melissa replied quickly. "I guess it would be better if that's what had happened, but no, it wasn't another girl. He loved me and only me. He wanted to spend the rest of his life with me. But then..."

"How did he die?"

Melissa realized that her heartache was obviously more evident than she had thought.

"Is it that easy to see?"

The server nodded. "I'm so sorry."

"It was a car wreck. About two months ago. I thought I was getting better but then a week or so ago I just took a turn for the worse. I don't think I'm going to be able to get over it. I thought I would, but now, well, I just don't know."

The server gave Melissa a sympathetic look, then placed her hand on her abdomen when she felt the baby move.

"How far along are you?" Melissa replied, eager to change the subject.

"About seven months. He's a real kicker, let me tell you." Melissa smiled as she looked at the server's extended abdomen, then back down into her coffee.

When she noticed the forlorn look on Melissa's face, the server decided she might be able to help the poor girl with her heartache.

"I don't mean to be nosey, but are you going to be staying in town? I mean, overnight maybe?"

Melissa smiled weakly. "Well, I hadn't really thought about it. But I need to get a little rest before I drive back to Asheville. It's a long drive. I don't think I could make it if I just got back in the car and tried to drive all the way home again. I'd probably end up falling asleep and driving into a bridge abutment."

The server chuckled. "We can't have that. And this little town has more to offer than you might think. You should stay a few days. You could rest up a little before you drive back to Asheville."

Melissa smiled and then noticed two people sitting in a booth across the diner. She wondered if they had been there when she walked in. One was an old man, and the other was a younger man who looked to be in his twenties. The server noticed her looking at the two men.

"The old man's name is Raymond. He runs the local towing business. Everybody in town calls him Ray," the server said with a grin, as if she had just let Melissa in on the town secret.

"The young guy sitting with him is my husband. The damn fool… I love him beyond words. He works at the Swamp Fox Inn. He manages the place. If you need a room for the night, he's the guy to see. I'll tell him to give you a good rate."

"Have you two lived in town very long?"

"Not really," replied the server. "A little less than a year, I guess. We just wanted to get away from big city life. My husband had family that lived here a long time ago, so we figured this town would be a good place to settle down." Melissa smiled but didn't reply. Used to a big city, she had always thought living in a small town where everyone knew each other would be nice.

The server smiled and tilted her head. "So how about staying in town? Just for tonight at least?"

Melissa considered the idea again, then turned and looked out the window at the small motel. "Yeah, I guess I could. I could use a good night's sleep."

The server tore the sheet out of her order pad. "Let me go put your order in with the kitchen and then I'll come back so we can talk.

I think a night in Solomon is just what you need."

Melissa was still not sure if staying in Solomon was a good idea but she knew she was tired and couldn't drive anymore without getting some rest. Maybe it would be okay to just stay today and maybe tonight. In the morning she could drive back to Asheville. Just as the server turned to walk away, Melissa spoke up.

"My name is Melissa, by the way."

The server gave her a smile. "I'm JoAnna," she said as she turned and walked away towards the kitchen.

Thank you for reading this novel.

Visit Dale on Goodreads at https://www.goodreads.com/djyoung

You are invited to leave a review at Amazon.com and share your thoughts about this book with other readers.

ABOUT THE AUTHOR

 Dale Young was born in North Carolina. His family has deep roots in the Blue Ridge Mountains, a dark and spooky land where superstitions about the dead run deep. The ghost stories and tales of wandering spirits passed down through his family over the years caused him many sleepless nights and inspired him to become a writer at an early age.

Dale writes horror and supernatural suspense novels set in the American South, where the souls of the dead seldom rest in peace. His novels are available in ebook format and in print.

www.ingramcontent.com/pod-product-compliance
Lightning Source LLC
Chambersburg PA
CBHW032134170626
46808CB00006B/2232